Into the Rabbit Hole

The Unbegun

In scientia fidei robur

Nisi qui habet scientiam in fide

Book 7

Books by Micah T. Dank

Into the Rabbit Hole *series*

Book 1: Beneath the Veil

Book 2: The Sacred Stones

Book 3: The Secret Weapon

Book 4: Pangaeas Pandemic

Book 5: The Hidden Archives

Book 6: The Final Type

Book 7: The Unbegun

Coming Soon!

Book 8: Nail in the Coffin

Into the Rabbit Hole

The Unbegun

Book 7

Micah T. Dank

SPEAKING VOLUMES, LLC
NAPLES, FLORIDA
2022

The Unbegun

ISBN 978-1-64540-764-5

To my best girlfriend since middle school,
Kim Gonzalez and her family Adrian, Jasmine
and Logan. Thank you for always keeping me in line.

My point, once again is not that those ancient people told literal stories and we are now smart enough to take them symbolically, but that they told them symbolically and we are now dumb enough to take them literally

—John Dominic Crossan.

Chapter One

Mecca, Saudi Arabia

"You know that Bible readers assume that the Tree of knowledge of good and evil was an apple tree, but in fact it was a fig tree. Years before, buddha became enlightened while sitting under a fig tree," Jahzeel said.

"I love it. Buddha also said 'Do not believe in traditions because they have been handed down for many generations. But after observation and analysis, when you find that anything agrees with reason and is conductive to the good and benefit of one and all, then accept it and live up to it,' " Syed said.

"Attention all. Please send all available police to the Kaaba. A man has lost his life within it. We need to do an investigation," the radio blasted.

"We're 5 minutes out. The Mabahith will take 40 minutes to get here. We have to be in and out. They're probably going to phone in the Mutawa," Jahzeel said.

They talked for a few moments in the hearse until they pulled up.

"Did you know that in the 1800's a beard was considered a sign that you were a lunatic or heretic?" Syed asked.

"That's amazing," Jahzeel said as they both applied their false beards. They were dressed in traditional police uniforms.

"I was wrong, we have 30 minutes until they get here. Let's go," Jahzeel said.

The men stepped out of their vehicle and went to the back of the hearse where they pulled out a bed on wheels and a bag to place the body in. They started making their way to the center of the Kaaba. Once they hit the inner circle of people, they started getting pushback.

"Who are you?" One man asked.

"Shurta, shurta! Please move," Jahzeel said.

The men made way for them. They walked through the people for a few moments until they came up to the door of the Kaaba.

"Everybody out!" Syed said.

The people started to leave. It was almost as if the dead body on the floor didn't bother any of them.

"Shut the doors Syed," Jahzeel said.

Syed shut the two doors to the Kaaba. One to leave and one to come in.

"We've got 25 minutes. Let's get to work," Jahzeel said.

They each grabbed one end section of the body, and put it on the gurney. They tried to close the body bag around him.

"Damn it, he's too tall. Quick, cover him with the white sheet," Syed said.

"You do that, I have to do my thing," Jahzeel said.

The Kaaba was gorgeous. The walls are white marble and green cloth on the upper half, signifying the flag which is Venus worship as Jahzeel had told Syed before. Jahzeel pulled out his laser cutter. State of the art. Could burn a tree down if need be. He made his way to the stone.

Jahzeel aimed the laser at the stone and started cutting into it. Brilliant lights were shooting out of it. This was no ordinary stone with no properties known to man. This came from a meteorite or some extra-terrestrial material. The Kaaba's black stone is often described as a fragmented dark rock. Its blackish color is speculation that this is due to how much it has been touched, along with the oils with which it is anointed. According to Muslim tradition, the stone was originally white, but turned black from being in a world where it absorbed humanity's sins. Muslims believe that Allah ordered the Kaaba to be constructed. The story goes that Abraham built the mosque with his oldest son, Ishmael, in the likeness of Allah's home in heaven. They also believe that the Kaaba stone was once part of the stones of Heaven. Jahzeel worked furiously on the stone for 10 minutes until finally a piece the size of two fists fell off. He caught it but dropped it on the floor since it was still burning hot.

"I hope you didn't break it," Syed said as he finished wrapping the body.

"It's fine, we have to go NOW!" Jahzeel yelped.

"Do you think this is taking us down the primrose path what we're doing or trying to do?" Syed asked.

"This is definitely going to shake things up for the worst before it gets better, that's for damn sure," Jahzeel replied.

Jahzeel hid the meteorite piece under the traditional white sheet covering of the body. He left a copy of the Koran on top of the body.

"It's now or never," Jahzeel said.

Syed opened the door and they started wheeling the body out; Jahzeel closed the door behind them. Most people gasped, and the gasps turned to anger. How dare someone murder someone in the holiest of buildings. They slowly made their way through the crowd and on their way out towards the hearse.

"We've got 10 minutes," Syed said, checking his watch.

"We'll be out of this country by then," Jahzeel laughed.

The people surrounding the Kaaba were looking curiously at the closed doors.

"What happened?!" One person asked Syed.

"Aintihar," Jahzeel replied.

"This man killed himself in a holy of holies. He will not be going to Jannah!" The man exasperated and turned around to go back to praying.

The two men kept walking for a few moments.

"Eventually they're going to open the door," Syed said.

Jahzeel turned around and noticed they started to crowd around it.

"Put some pep in your step boy or we're dead men," Jahzeel said.

They started pushing faster. As they were about 200 feet from the hearse they saw people opening the door and pouring in. A few seconds later there were some loud shreakings. One man ran out and pointed to us, no doubt noticing a big chunk of the stone was missing. All at once they gathered like a white clothed swarm and started running after us.

"Hurry up!" Syed screamed.

They made it to the hearse and loaded the body in. They hopped in the car, ripped off their beards and Jahzeel took off down the road, just as the police were arriving on their heels.

"That was too close," Syed exasperated.

"We made it out alive, that's all that matters," Jahzeel said. "Go get the stone."

Syed wiggled his way into the back and took the stone. It was a lot heavier than he thought it would be. He'd never seen anything like it before.

After driving for 45 minutes, they pulled down a side road. It was starting to get dark out. Jahzeel pulled out his laser again and carefully seared the VIN number of the vehicle off. Then he joined Syed in the back. He grabbed a duffle bag and opened it; it had their change of clothes. Both men changed quickly and put the police uniforms back into the duffle bag. Syed got out of the car and ripped both license plates off and switched them with false ones. He then grabbed the two fake beards and twisted them into a giant knot. The men got out of the car and Syed opened the gas tank and shoved the beards into it while Jahzeel grabbed the two suitcases.

"Do you want to do the honors?" Jazheel asked in a laughing matter.

"Just do it already, we have a plane to catch," Syed said.

"Suit yourself," Jahzeel said as he shrugged his shoulders. He took the laser out once more and lit the beards on fire. Both men started running down the streets. As they turned the corner and took a few steps, they heard a giant explosion. Burning cars was nothing new in this area of the world, Jahzeel thought. They had both been wearing white gloves the entire time in the car. Jahzeel was confident there was no way it could trace back to them. After they got far enough away, they dropped the hot license plates in the garbage. They turned a corner a few more blocks down and hopped into a rental vehicle. Jahzeel got in the driver's seat after they put the suitcases in the trunk.

"The stone is in one of these, correct?" Jahzeel quizzed.

"Of course," Syed replied.

The men made their way down to the Airport. They were about to have a long commute. They also had no idea the chain of events they had just set off.

All truth passes through three stages. First, it is ridiculed. Second, it is violently opposed. Third, it is accepted as being self-evident. —Arthur Schopenhauer

Chapter Two

Rue de Bonaparte, Paris, France

"Alright, we're all set up. Let's get to work," Jahzeel said as he set down the stone.

The two men went to their makeshift lab and began furiously working. After about five hours Syed stepped back.

"I've got the worst headache," Syed said.

"It's all that nitric oxide you take. You know that's basically Viagra, right? Headaches are incredibly common. All that just to get a perpetual pump when you work out. Is it worth it? There's a pharmacy downstairs across the street. Go get something," Jahzeel said.

"Yeah, I could use some Tylenol, my head is killing me," Syed decried.

"They don't sell Tylenol in France Syed, it's banned throughout the entire country," Jahzeel advised.

"Well, shit. What am I supposed to get?" he asked.

"Relax, codeine is legal here and without a prescription," Jahzeel replied.

"Awesome. So much for having a few drinks later tonight," Syed replied.

"No drinks, we have too much to do. Also, you do know that cocktails were invented so that the juice could hide the taste of dead animals in bootleg liquor, right?" Jahzeel laughed.

"That's disgusting, and I'm going to pretend you didn't say that. I'll be back," Syed said.

Syed walked down the street and picked up a bottle of codeine and decided to take a short walk down the street and back. He hadn't been gone for 25 minutes before he got a call from Jahzeel on his burner.

"Get up here immediately. I think we're close," Jahzeel said as he hung up.

Syed rushed back to the apartment and raced upstairs. The French sure don't love their elevators.

"What is it?" Syed asked.

"Look!" Jahzeel squealed as he pointed to the table.

There it was, pure as day. A piece of gold the size of a one and a half fists. They lost some of the material during the final process.

"The fear of death is the beginning of slavery," Jahzeel touted.

"Indeed. Also, in Bhutan, most of the buildings have erect penises painted on them. They believe that an erect penis keeps away evil people, spirits, and gossip" Syed said. "What now?"

"Now, we get it tested. There's a jewelry store a few miles away.

Suddenly there was a knock on the door. The two men looked at each other. Syed pulled his gun out and walked gingerly towards the door.

"Who is it?" he asked.

"C'est Fedex. Ouvrez s'il vous plait," The Fed Ex employee said.

"Je ne peux pas maintenant," Syed said.

"Vous avez un accent, parlez-vous Anglais?" The man said.

"Oui, I mean, yes," Syed said.

"OK, look I have a ton of shit to do, I'm just leaving it here. Take care," the man said.

"Wait, please leave us 10 boxes at the door," Syed said.

"Seriously? I can't just leave them." The Fed Ex employee said.

"It's fine, just do it," Syed said as he slipped 100 Euro under the door. "Just say you got robbed."

"Incroyable," he said as his footsteps became fainter. After a minute or two they heard the footsteps again. Then it sounded like someone dropped a package Ace Ventura style on the doorstep. The two men sat there quietly waiting to hear the steps fade, which they eventually did. Jahzeel went to open the door while Syed put his gun away. He opened the door and brought the boxes in. Once inside, he opened the box and lifted the item out.

"I can't believe we were able to get this," Jahzeel said.

"Can it be?" Syed asked.

"Look," Jahzeel said.

Sure enough, it was right there in front of them. It was a pyramid shaped cut of the Benben stone. The other two men were able to pull it off somehow. They even cut the part with hieroglyphics on it.

"Well, so much for leaving. Show me exactly what I missed," Syed said.

"Let's get to work," Jahzeel said.

30 hours later

The two men looked at the table. They shook their heads in disbelief.

"Can it really be?" Syed asked.

"It appears so," Jahzeel said.

"The works of Pythagoras, Galileo, Newton, Plato, Aristotle, Copernicus. Yet it is us brother that figured it out. We have to get these checked as soon as possible," Syed yelped excitedly.

"We need to fill out the packages now," Jahzeel said.

"No wait, we need to make sure. Let's go to the car, they're still open for another 90 minutes," Syed said.

"True story," Jahzeel said.

The two men took the two pieces of gold off the table and brought them to the car. Syed jumped in the driver's side as he was accustomed to driving in France.

25 minutes later

"Alright, let's do this; it's now or never," Jahzeel said as he exited the car.

The two men walked into the jewelry store. A man from behind the counter came up to them.

"Hello, what can I do for you gentlemen?" The jeweler asked.

"Hello, we'd like to sell these, could you please give us a price?" Syed asked as he handed them two gumball sized balls of gold.

"Oh my, let me take a look," the jeweler said as put his magnifying monacle on and walked into the back with them.

Jahzeel and Syed sat there with their hands in their pockets looking around the place. This jewelry shop looked like it had seen better days, but they held a small fortune within itself. Jahzeel wondered why they didn't fix the place up. The two men looked at each other and Jahzeel was about to open his mouth and ask Syed a question when the man came running out from the back.

"WHERE DID YOU GET THESE?!" The man harbored.

"Why does it matter?" Jahzeel asked nervously.

"I've never seen anything like this. This one is purer than 24k gold, and this one is even better. Who did you steal this from?" The jeweler asked.

"We didn't steal it," Syed fumed.

"I don't believe you. I'm calling the police," the jeweler said.

"Look, we don't want any trouble, just give them back to us, and we'll be on our way," Jahzeel pleaded.

"You two are not going anywhere," the jeweler said as he pulled out a gun and aimed it at them and hit his alarm.

Jahzeel and Syed looked at each other with worry on their faces. They had to think fast.

"I don't want to have to hurt you, but I will if I have to," Syed said.

The jeweler laughed. Syed kept him engaged while Jahzeel slowly reached into his back pocket and pulled out his laser. In one fluid motion, he pulled his right hand up and aimed it at the jeweler's hands. The burn from the laser was extraordinary and the jeweler yelped and dropped his gun on the floor. Syed grabbed the two balls off the counter and the two made a run for the door. Once they got outside, they jumped in the car and Syed peeled off, the jeweler right behind them with his gun shooting the back window of the car out. Syed turned the corner.

"We're fucked," Jahzeel said.

"Relax, we got this," Syed said.

"They have cameras in there, and there's a camera outside; they probably know what car we are in and the license plates," Jahzeel said.

"So we'll ditch the car and get another one," Syed said.

"This isn't good, they have our faces on camera and we weren't wearing our beards. You know in France in court you are guilty until proven innocent, right?" Jahzeel asked.

"We've got to speed up the timeline, we've got to send the Fed Ex boxes out and get the hell out of France," Syed replied. "First, let's ditch the car."

Syed drove down a side rode and parked the car; he jumped out of it and grabbed Jahzeel's laser. He cut out one of the bricks from the pathway and brought it into the car. He tossed the laser back to Jahzeel.

"I'm going to drop you off at the apartment, start prepping the samples and fill out the paperwork," Syed said.

"What are you going to do?" Jahzeel asked.

"I'm ditching the car," Syed said.

Syed dropped Jahzeel off at the apartment, Jahzeel ran upstairs and started filling out the envelopes to send them out. Syed had asked for 10 but they only needed 9. Until Jahzeel remembered the plan. If something were to go wrong, send a sample to Graham Newsdon. He would know what to do.

15 minutes later Syed showed up at the apartment.

"What took you so long?" Jahzeel asked.

"I told you I was ditching the car," Syed replied.

"What did you do with it?" Jahzeel asked.

"I drove it into the Seine," Syed said.

Jahzeel looked at him blankly.

"I panicked and it was right there. That's why I took the brick from the road, to put on the gas pedal. I don't think anybody saw us, plus the Seine is super close to our apartment anyway. I also dropped off the item at the wall of locks," Syed said.

"Good, Jahzeel said as he put the finishing touches on the boxes. He then took them one by one and put them into the duffle back, careful to leave a small piece of the BenBen and the Kaaba stone on the table, as well as one small ball of gold.

They walked out the front door and hailed a taxi. They went to the local Fed Ex and sent the packages out with a fake address on the return. Then they hailed another cab and went to the airport, never to be seen again.

Truth is treason in an empire of lies —George Orwell

Chapter Three

2 weeks later

"Hannah come in here and get James. I'm about to go live and he's chewing on a computer wire," I pleaded.

"Oh Jesus, JAMES PIERCE! Get your butt in here," Hannah called out.

I turned and watched my son with the wire in his mouth freeze like a deer in a headlight, spit out the wire, stand up and walk out of the room.

"You know that daddy has to do work. How do you think we keep the lights on here?" Hannah asked James.

"I'm sorry mama," James replied.

"Sorry baby, have fun. I know this guy is a huge deal on the internet," Hannah said as she gave me a kiss then locked the door from the inside and shut it.

"Sorry about that brother," I said to the computer.

"It's all good baby; here at the Conspiracy Castle we know all about this kind of stuff. I have five cats myself," The host said.

"Did you just say five cats?" I asked bewildered.

"Hold on, I'm just setting everything up, we're going live in 30 seconds. Are you ready to go bud?" he asked.

"Ready, ready," I replied

"OK, so I'm going to play my intro music, then do the intro segment and bring you on," He replied, as he put up three fingers, then two, then one. I took a sip of my diet peach Snapple.

After about 90 seconds he came on the screen.

"Ladies and gentlemen, boys and girls, children of all ages, welcome to THE Conspiracy Castle, I'm your conspiracy asshole, Prime Time 99 Alex Stein, rise and shine, on the grind, all the time, I'd like to give a very special shoutout to my guest tonight. You've seen him on Aquastream, read about him in books, and soon to be on an arena tour talking about his work, deep into the conspiracy world, Graham Newsdon. Welcome Graham to the Conspiracy Castle," Alex said.

"It's great to finally meet you, I've heard a lot about you," I replied.

"That's right baby, you know Prime Time 99 Alex Stein gets the glory, it's all mine. So, I have to ask you first and foremost. I notice that you never talk politics. Is that because you're afraid of cancel culture?" He asked as he took a bite of his pizza. I'd never seen a host eat on the air, but I felt rather relaxed because of it.

"Wait, is that Alfredo pizza, with pineapple?!" I asked incredulously.

"Let me chime in on a dime, I'm Prime Time 99. Eating the all-time best foods at lunchtime. Hell freakin yeah this is Alfredo pizza with pineapple. You know, I've got to be careful though. I'm not as in shape as I was in college. Still on my grind though. So, back to it. Oh wait, Skybear wants to say hello. Hold on," Alex said as he bent over and picked up one of his cats.

"Wait, are you not wearing pants either?" I asked laughingly.

"It's playtime for prime time all the time, Graham. I'm in Texas, so you know it gets hot here," Alex said.

"I know, but you're wearing a 3 piece suit top, I dunno, it just confused me," I replied.

"Skybear say hi!" He replied. "You know, when you have five cats that constantly need attention, it gets very hard at the Conspiracy Castle and the Conspiracy Household. I'm almost sure that I have toxoplasmosis. It's turned me into a crazy cat lady," Alex replied.

My mind shot back to my book Pangaeas Pandemic, where I retold the story about the global flu vaccine and the jellyfish protein, and we had to infect millions and millions of people with toxo in order to get them through until their immune system fought it off.

"Back to business though. So what about cancel culture vultures. Is that why you never share your political views?" Alex asked as he took a giant swig out of some no name soda brand.

"Well Alex, to be honest with you, when I first got my publishing deal, the publicist that I got told me that if you get political, you'll alienate half of your audience, so curb the politics. Now, because I talk about hidden Bible codes and that the Bible is just an encoded Astrology book, people assume that I'm on the left and waging a war on the religious right. While it's true that I have a problem with 'Holy Book literalists,' I'm neither on the right nor the left. I've been on the left, then I was on the right, now I just hate them both equally. I just want to be left alone. But late night hosts keep trying to get me to go on their shows and get me to commit one way or another. I just don't have time for that. You know, when I first started out talking about my work and my books which are about 95% truth to what happened to me, the only people that would give me a platform was the Twitter conspiracy community. I built a rather large following this way, plus my Aquastream videos as well. That's why I keep doing these types of podcasts and tv shows, that don't make me jump into any of the bullshit in politics," I said as I was cut off.

"WOW, sorry Graham, I don't mean to interrupt but Lazarus one of my Patreons just super chatted $100 to the Conspiracy Castle, thank you so much Lazarus, you know with the supply chain being all fucked up, this is going to go a long way towards feeding my cats and maybe this blonde bombshell I have coming over later tonight. Your question to Graham is 'Do you ever miss the adrenaline or rush of running around the world, saving it and ruining these elite globalists lives?' " Alex asked.

"Well, to be honest, wait a second. Did I hear you right? You're going to feed your date cat food tonight?" I asked Alex.

"Graham, I'm Prime Time 99 in the nighttime. I'm a legend at this. You know I used to work on a dating show a few years back. I'm working overtime on the paradigm. Don't worry about what she eats," He replied.

"I mean, I see what you're eating now, and it's disgusting," I replied.

"No it's not. Graham, fly down to Dallas and I'll show you how to live brother!" He replied.

"Right. Anyway, to answer his question; The last five years have been a little quiet, but it's good. I have a son now and I'm starting an arena tour in a few months, so I've been working up some notes on how I'm going to approach that," I replied.

"Are you doing Dallas?" Alex asked. "Because Prime Time 99 Alex Stein rise and shine, on the grind, would LOVE to take you around Dallas afterwards.

"Um, I'm not sure yet, I haven't gotten the dates. I know that I'm doing Boston though," I replied.

"Is that where you still live?" he asked.

"Yeah, it is. We've since moved, and because of my public status now, I can't really tell people where I live, but I'm still in the general area." I replied.

"Let's talk about your friends. Jackson, the brick shithouse physics nerd, Rosette the snarky psychologist, Jean the rich boy and Larisa who heads up an IT firm now. How are they all doing? Also, is everything that you wrote in your book series true? You guys are like a well-oiled machine, holy shit!" Alex replied.

I laughed and reflected for a minute. "You know, I never thought about it really, but we've needed all our expertise to get things done," I replied.

"Now, I know that you've lost some people along the way. Let me just say that I'm sorry for your loss," Alex said in a rare moment of brotherly connection.

"I appreciate that man, you know, sometimes when you make an omelet, you've got to break a few eggs, and I suppose that NP and Josh had to pay the price. It's funny because when my books got turned into cinema,

I thought to myself, there's no way that I'm going to be able to survive this," I said.

"It's true. Do you know how many people that expose corruption and evil go on Twitter or Aquastream and tell people that 'they would never kill themselves,' and end up getting killed anyway, and nobody questions it," Alex replied.

"Yeah, that's why I don't bother doing that. I'm just going to keep doing what I'm doing and making sure that people KNOW the truth behind things, and if one day something should happen to . . ." I got cut off.

"WOW!! Alex Steins Dick just super chatted $150 dollars. Wow. I mean, I know that Prime Time 99, Alex Stein has a very nice dick, but I never thought I'd hear from it on Patreon. Alex Steins Dick, whoever you are, thank you so much.

I laughed. I thought of my friend Chrissie Mayr who I filmed that scene with in the second movie, has a Twitter follower 'Chrissie Mayr's boobs' who basically posts about how they want to be 'freed' all the time. Some people have too much time on their hands. I've NEVER seen something like that about me, but then again, I am always busy with my kid and my wife.

"So what now?" I asked.

"What now is we're going to bring some people into video chat to ask you questions, if you're ok with that," Alex replied.

"OK, I'm cool with that," I replied.

"Wait, before we do that, I have to ask you. Have you heard about what's going on in the news?" Alex asked.

"You mean with the gold that they can't figure out how it got so pure?" I asked.

"Yeah. So for those of you who haven't been paying attention the last 7 days, apparently nine balls of gold the size of a Godiva chocolate had been sent to various central banks around the world, and even the queen got one. This gold is supposedly greater than 24k gold, which is just insane. Hold on a second, they're talking about it on tv. Graham, just hold on a second," Alex said as he whizzed around his computer and brought another screen into our view with the news.

This gold that has appeared out of no-where has set the owners of the central banks on fire. Apparently, this is the purest gold that has ever been found, and due to its discovery or should I say, brought to light in the world, it's making major disruptions in the economic systems. Old gold has dropped

in price dramatically, where this new gold has shot up to astronomical pricing. Where did this gold come from? What will happen to people who've invested in precious metals? Silver is still holding strong. For now. As always, this is Jennifer Polizzi reporting live. More to come when we have it.

"What?! Gold is dropping significantly? What is going on Graham?" Alex asked.

"I have no idea, but I'm glad it's not my problem," I replied.

"Two weeks ago, it was the murder at the Kaaba that turned the Islamic world upside down and now this. It's like they never run out of bullshit to feed us." Alex said. "Anyway, do you want to take some live chats and questions?"

"Yeah, I guess we could do that for sure. I think that . . ." I trailed as I heard a knock on the door. "Hold on a second Alex, my wife's at the door."

"No problem, Graham. We're talking with Graham Newsdon everyone!" Alex said.

I opened the door and my wife was standing there.

"Hi hunny, James was playing with this. It came for you," Hannah said.

"What is it?" I asked.

"You tell me Graham," She replied.

"I looked at the packaging. It had a forwarding address, no doubt a fake one. There was a single thumbprint of blood on the bottom of the Fed Ex packaging. A feeling sank in my stomach.

"Thanks love, go take care of James, I'm almost done here," I replied.

She gave me a kiss and locked the door behind her.

"What was that?" Alex asked.

"It's nothing, I just got a package that's all," I said as I started opening it off camera.

I opened the box which was taped very tightly shut and my eye grew wide. After opening several layers of packaging in the center of it was a bright gold ball that was almost glowing the size of an oreo. There was also a sealed letter in the package. Alex must have noticed my facial cues change drastically.

"What did you get?" Alex asked.

"Don't worry about it. Listen Alex, I have to go," I replied.

"What did you get? Is it related to something we've talked about today?" he asked.

I stared back blankly.

"It is isn't it! Come on, tell the Conspiracy Castle Nation what it is," He replied.

"I'm sorry, I have to go. We'll do this another time," I said.

"Alright, ladies and gentlemen boys and girls, children of all ages, this is the Conspiracy Castle, and I'm your one and only Conspiracy Asshole. Thank you for tuning in today, catch me later on tonight as I go over the week's news with you.' He said as he signed off.

I stared at this ball for a few minutes. Finally, my wife knocked on the door as I tore the letter open. She opened it. She saw the news on in the background and was familiar with what was happening with the gold. When she saw me holding the ball and the letter, her face turned pale.

"This can't be happening again," she said.

"I think it is," I replied.

"Why us? Why is it always us?" she pleaded.

"I don't know, but we've got to get everyone over. It came with a letter," I admonished.

"I'll put James down and we'll call together," she said.

She turned and walked down the hall to get our son. I sat back down on the chair and looked at this ball. In my wildest dreams, I couldn't imagine what was about to happen to all of us.

If you look at the people in your circle and you don't get inspired, you don't have a circle, you have a cage
—Nipsey Hussle

Chapter Four

"Hey Hannah, take a look at this," I said as I handed her the letter that was in the package.

"Here James, hand that to mommy," she replied.

James handed her the letter. She opened it, shaking her head and scanned the letter. Her eyes opened wide as she looked at me, then looked at the letter, then looked at me again.

"Graham, I thought we were over all of this. Where did this come from?" she asked.

"It was in the box that you brought to me earlier. As well as this," I said as I placed the gold ball on the table. Her eyes grew wider.

"Is that?" She began.

"Gold," I replied

"Just like the banks received on T.V.?" she asked

I nodded my head.

"Well, we have to return it. We can't have any part of this," she said.

"Hear me out a minute," I replied.

"Graham, we have a FAMILY now. We've been trying for a second one for a few months now and James is about to go into kindergarten, and I can't allow this," Hannah said.

"OK I get it. Just, let me take this to a jeweler and see what they say. You know Will down the road. I'll just see what he says and be back in 45 minutes tops," I said.

Hannah looked at me and crossed her arms. Never a good sign. She then rolled her eyes as loudly as she could and looked at me. Her face changed into acceptance, and she slumped.

"No more than an hour," she demanded.

"OK," I said.

I stood up from the table and ruffled James's curly blonde hair. I have no idea where he got the curly or the blonde from. I swear she must be having an affair with the Amazon delivery driver or something. I went into the garage and hopped in the car. Within a moment or two I was off.

I arrived at the Jewelers a few minutes later. I got out of the car and walked inside. There was one person ahead of me who was buying an engagement ring. Good for him. He was just being rung up. Shortly thereafter, Will came to the window to greet me.

"Graham, how are you my friend. How's the wife and kid?" he asked.

"Things are just peachy, until this showed up at my doorstep today," I replied.

"What is it?" he asked.

"You tell me," I replied.

I handed him the little ball of gold and he looked at it as his eyes grew wide.

"Could you wait right here for me for a minute?" He asked as he put on his contraption to take a closer look at it.

"I'll be here," I replied.

"Good," he said.

Will walked into the back room where there was even more light than there was in the jewelry shop. I looked around for a few moments. I got Hannah's engagement ring and our wedding bands from here. I bought James a bracelet for when he turns 18. We were close. I looked in the back. Something was off. Will was marching furiously back at me.

"Where did you get this Graham?" he asked.

"What does it matter?" I asked.

"Graham," he began as he turned on the news.

If anybody has any further information on where these gold balls came from, please

report it to your local authority. So far nine have been recovered, and from what we know there's a tenth, maybe an eleventh out there. It is a matter of national security for you to speak up if you have any information. As always, this is Jennifer Polizzi, signing off.

"Graham, I'm supposed to turn this and you into the authorities," Will said as he looked at the ball then back at me, "But I'm not going to do that," he said as he handed me the ball back. "Go home Graham."

"Wait, can you at least tell me what we are looking at?" I asked.

Will sighed as he looked at me "Are you familiar with 24k gold?" he asked.

I shook my head no.

"It's supposed to be the purest gold there is out there. This is twice as pure, at LEAST twice as pure. I've never seen something so perfect in my life. A go-diva chocolate bar is about 1 ounce. Its current value would be almost 1900 dollars. This ball is about 3 ounces. Its value would be about 5700, but this gold I would say is at least quadruple that. Honestly, I don't think that anybody has ever seen something like this before. Go ahead, take this home. I'll erase the security footage, I think my apprentice may have seen this. Go Graham!" He exclaimed.

I shook my head and took the ball and went out the door. I jumped in the car and sped off. What was going on here?

I got home and went into the kitchen where Hannah was loading the dishwasher.

"Babe, you're never going to believe this," I began.

"No, YOU'RE never going to believe this. This shit is on the news Graham. What are we involved in?" she asked.

"I have no idea yet, but I think it has to do with the letter we got," I replied.

"I have this sick feeling in my stomach hun all over again. I'm assuming you want to call them up?" she asked.

I nodded.

"Let me just put James to bed and then I'll be in there. DON'T call them without me," she said.

I agreed.

I went downstairs to the man cave my wife had in-sisted on building for me and queued up Jean, Larisa, Rosette and Jackson. After about 10 minutes she came downstairs.

"Alright, call them," she said

I video called them. After about 30 seconds, Jean and Larisa came up on the screen.

"Hey guys, how are you?" Larisa asked.

"We've had a very interesting day," Hannah replied.

"Oh?" Larisa asked.

"What happened mes amis?" Jean replied

"Have you been following the news about that new gold that came out?" I asked.

"Yeah, that's crazy. Economists are already saying how devastating this will be to the global economy. They say that all the gold that's ever been mined, if you piled it an inch thick, would only run two Manhattan blocks. If that becomes obsolete, then what? Silver? It would crash the world's economies. They're still doing studies on it right now, but as far as we can gather, this is absolutely pure, no blemishes. How did nine central banks suddenly become in possession of this?" Larisa asked.

"Hey guys, how are you?" Rosette asked.

"Hey girl, what's for dinner? Me?" Larisa asked and winked.

Rosette giggled, "No that's dessert," she said.

"Don't tease me with a good time girl, so what's that in your hand?" Larisa asked.

"Ugh, it's a shake. I've been doing a 2 week juice cleanse like I'm preparing for the biggest anal scene of my life in the morning. So, what's up?" Rosette asked.

"We're talking about how those nine banks got that ball of pure gold earlier, Larisa replied.

"Yeah, I heard about that while I was on the Peloton. That's crazy. They're saying it'll crash everything if it turns out to be real," Rosette.

"They still can't figure out how the nine banks got a hold of them. They just magically showed up one day," Jackson retorted between enormous bites of salmon and green beans.

"Not nine guys, ten," I replied as I held up the ball to the camera.

Everybody stopped what they were doing and stared at me.

"Where the fuck did you get that Newsdon?" Rosette asked.

"It was sent to me. I was doing Alex Steins podcast today and Hannah handed me the mail. It also came with this," I said as Hannah handed me the letter.

"And what is that exactly?" Jackson asked.

"I'll read it to you. You'll never believe me if I just tell you," I said.

In the plot of the last great King of the Louvre you will find no Invalids. Raised to the highest, there is a magic station. To access it you must seek the lock of Rofocale sitting amongst many other. You must continue the decoded work of the ancient scholars and collapse the oldest currency

Everybody stopped.

"Graham, it's been five years. Why would someone come to us now? What's the point?" Larisa asked.

"I have no idea, but I can't just ignore this. I went to our Jeweler and he basically told me he had to turn me in for being in possession of that. He said it's worth over 20,000 an ounce," I said.

"So should I dust off the plane?" Jean asked.

"Not yet. First we need to figure this out," I replied.

"Well, it's France," Rosette said.

"What?" Hannah asked.

"King of the Louvre, the Louvre is in France. Road trip?" Rosette asked.

"Hold on, we've got a son now, it's not that simple," Hannah said.

"Leave him with my parents. James LOVES his grandparents," Rosette said.

"We need to think about this," Hannah said.

"Wait, turn up Blur real quick, he's talking about the gold," Larisa said.

I'm telling you people, the issue at the Kaaba is connected to the issue with the BenBen stone. It's too coincidental that these pieces of these ancient artifacts go missing days apart. Why is nobody talking about this? Oh, it's because they're obsessed with this new gold that came out. To me, it's just a psyop in order to crash the dollar in order to bring in the New World Order, one world currency and to . . .

I turned the TV off.

"What do you think? Should I reach out to my parents? Rosette asked.

I looked at Hannah, she looked at me. "Fine," Hannah said. "I'll go pack for us. Jean when are we leaving?"

"I can have it ready at this point by midnight. We'll sleep on the way there," He replied.

Hannah looked at me "You're lucky I love you, asshole," she said as she gave me a kiss and tugged on my beard.

"I'll bring the box it came in, in case there are any clues with it," I replied.

"Alright Graham, my mom is coming over to get James in about 45 minutes." Rosette said.

"Guys, we're in and out of France, I'm so over these things," I said.

"Agreed," Jackson replied.

I turned off the video chat. They would all meet at my place since I was closest to Logan out of all of them. In and out of France. Nothing could have been farther from the truth.

The books that the world calls immoral are the books that show the world its own shame —Oscar Wilde

Chapter Five

The flight was uneventful. I left the ball of gold in our house hidden safely behind our false wall outlet safe. We pulled into CDG airport at about 1pm. We got out and had a car waiting for us.

"Where to?" The driver asked.

"The Louvre," Jean replied.

"Alright," the driver said.

We relaxed in the limo ride over.

"Napoleon was the last great King of the Louvre. The Louvre is actually where he lived when he was alive. There are tours that take you around his facilities, with all original furniture and all. C'est incroyable," Jean said.

We pulled up outside the Louvre pyramid. Jean slipped the driver 100 Euros and told him to wait there. We made our way inside. Once inside, Jean gave his card and got us all tickets for the tour.

"I've always wanted to visit this place, but I never had the ability to," Larisa said.

"I want to see the Mona Lisa!" Rosette squealed.

"Guys, we're here for a reason. Remember, in and out," I said.

They looked disappointed but they all understood.

We walked for a bit until we got to the section of Napoleon. We took the tour, Larisa taking pictures of everything, and I mean everything.

"Guys, I don't know about you, but I don't see a 'magic station' anywhere," Hannah replied.

"Yeah, I'm not too sure of this, hold on a second," Jean said as he walked up to the tour guide and whispered something in French to her. She shook her head no and laughed and Jean made his way back.

"Apparently there's no such thing as a magic station anywhere," Jean slumped.

"Alright, well Larisa took a ton of pictures, let's find a place to sit and go through them all," I replied.

We went downstairs and found a large table to sit at. One by one, we went through all of Larisa's pictures, zooming in and out. Nothing.

"Well, I guess this is a dead end. Let's go home, I miss my baby," Hannah said.

"Hold on a second," I said as I pulled out the letter again.

In the plot of the last great King of the Louvre you will find no Invalids. Raised to

the highest, there is a magic station. To access it you must seek the lock of Rofocale sitting amongst many other. You must continue the decoded work of the ancient scholars and collapse the oldest currency.

"There, see, right there. In the PLOT of the last great King of the Louvre. Napoleon's plot. His grave. Jean! Where is he buried?" I asked.

"He's buried right here in Paris," Jean replied.

"Alright, let's at least see this out," I said.

"Agreed," Jackson replied.

"Fine by my blood," Rosette said.

We got back in the car and Jean told the driver where to go. It wasn't that long of a ride at all, took about 20 minutes with traffic. Once we got there, we got out of the vehicle and took in the giant Hotel.

We walked inside and asked someone where we could find the tomb. They pointed us to the right direction. Within moments, we were standing in front of the tomb. It was unlike any tomb I'd ever seen.

"Alright guys, Larisa, take pictures. Look around the sarcophagus and see if you can find anything." I said.

We all looked around it, but it was plain maroon and nothing on it. I slumped back annoyed. There has to be something here, I just know it.

"Guys, check these statues surrounding it. These are known as 'Napoleon's Angels.' There might be something there for us," Jean replied.

We took another 30 minutes wandering around the room, there was absolutely nothing. No clues, nothing. We were all starting to get frustrated, until I took another look at the letter.

"Wait guys, the letter," I said.

"What about it?" Rosette asked.

"In the plot of the last great King of the Louvre, you will find no Invalids. Raised to the highest," I began as I was cut off.

"We're in the wrong place. Merde!" Jean replied

"What do you mean?" I asked.

"You will find no Invalids. C'est emplacement is called 'The Invalides,' the letter says you will find no invalids. I do have an idea though," Jean said.

We all looked at him with a dumb look on our faces.

"Well, what?!" Jackson asked.

"Calm down big man. Listen, the word plot can also mean a piece of land. If it's not here and it's not at the Louvre, it must be at his home plot," Jean replied.

"What do you mean?" I asked.

"Rue de Bonaparte." It's a street not far from le Seine. We need to go now," Jean said as he motioned us to leave and get back in the car.

We got back in the car and took a short ride passing the Seine along the way. Finally, he made a right onto Rue de Bonaparte. The street was eloquent. Stones, very antiquated. Reminded me of some streets I've been to in Boston. We got out of the vehicle and stood around.

"Alright, now what Solex?" Larisa asked.

"Just let me think a minute," Jean said as he rubbed his temples.

"Are we just going to try and open every door on this block?" Hannah asked.

"Jackson could just kick them down," Larisa said.

"Not a chance guys, even I couldn't break these. They're modern-day locks on very heavy very old doors," Jackson said as he assessed the area.

I started pacing around, looking at the letter while everyone argued. After a few minutes, I had an epiphany.

"Raised to the highest," I said and trailed off.

"What are you thinking baby?" Hannah asked.

"Being raised is a freemason term. The highest would be the 33rd degree," I said.

"So, what does that mean?" Rosette asked.

"Is there a 33 on this block?" I asked.

Jackson looked at me and took off down the road. After about 30 seconds, we saw him coming back. "It's about 6 houses down," he said.

"How did you put that together Newsdon?" Rosette asked.

"Napoleon was supposedly a freemason. There are a lot of conflicting details regarding this, some say he was, some said that what he said about them proves that he wasn't. But could have also been a deterrence from people knowing the truth." I replied.

We got to the door. 33 Rue de Bonaparte. There was a key lock and what looked like a thumb print scanner as well.

"Fucking great," Jackson said.

"Wait guys," I said as I ran back to the car, took out the box and brought it back to them. I flipped it upside down and revealed the bloody thumbprint. I tore the box and was left with the thumbprint. I placed it on the scanner and a red horizontal line ran up and down. The light then turned green and I tried to open the door, but it was still locked on top.

"Damn it," I said.

"Let me see that letter," Jean said.

I handed it over to him. He read the letter a few times to himself.

"I think I know what this is about," Jean said.

"Well, don't keep us guessing Jean! What is it?! Larisa yelped.

"Lucifuge Rofocale. According to the Grand Grimoire is in charge of Hell's government and treasury by order of Lucifer. Now, the treasury are angels that take people back in if they try and escape, but the treasury can also mean our modern treasury, which has been disturbed by the gold. The 'lock' that sits amongst others. Not far from here, there is a metal gate, which people write their names on and lock to the gate forever. It's a tradition. I bet that's where we have to go," Jean thumped.

"I'm fine with you knowing that, but why do you know so much about demonology?" Larisa asked worried.

"Because I'm bad, and I need to be punished, mon Cherie," Jean said.

"Alright you two, enough. Jean, can we walk it, or should we take a car?" I asked.

"Up to you," he replied.

"Alright, let's take the car, I'm still jet lagged over here guys," Rosette said.

We piled into the car and drove over to the bridge where we saw hundreds of locks on a wall.

"This should only take a few hours," Jackson said.

Jackson and I got out of the car and walked over to the locks. We started tediously scanning them one by one. After about twenty minutes the driver honked. Jackson promptly stood up and gave him the finger and went back down to looking.

"Here! I think I found it!" I said.

We both looked at the padlock. It was stronger than the others that were attached. Sure enough, it said ROFOCALE on it. I turned it around and there was a key attached to the back of it. I removed the key and started smiling and waved to everyone to come over. Everyone escaped the car and came over to where we were. I handed the key over to Rosette.

"Alright guys, maybe we should walk back. It's not that far and I don't want the driver putting anything together about what we're doing," I said as I was interrupted by Hannah.

"Uh, Graham," Hannah began.

"What? I asked.

"There aren't any markings on this key," she said.

"I know, there's not supposed to. We got it off the back of the Rofocale lock," I said.

"No genius, LOOK. It's not a functioning key," Rosette said.

Sure enough, I looked at the key and there were no bumps and ridges to indicate it was a proper key. My heart sank to my ass.

"Well, this is great. Now what?" Jean asked.

I looked back over the wall of locks. There were way too many to check. We had to figure something out.

I searched the other locks the best I could. As I was about to give up, I saw one that caught my eye.

ALGOL

I smiled and picked it up and lifted it upside down since it was still attached to the wall. There was another key on the back of it. This one HAD ridges.

"How the hell did you?" Hannah began.

"This is astrology. Algol is known as the demon star. I figured with Rofocale being evil to begin with, another one would be here too. Algol is where we get the evil name in Batman 'Ras AlGhoul.' " I said.

"Well that's great, but can we go back now? I'm actually getting cold standing by the water," Jackson said.

"Since when are you ever cold?" Hannah asked.

"Since right now," he replied.

Jean tipped the driver another 100 Euros and sent him on his way. We started walking back. Along the way we saw a series of plain white vans with the bubble window in the back.

"Don't bother them guys," Jean said.

"What do you mean?" I asked.

"Those are prostitution vans," he replied.

"What?!" I asked incredulously.

"This is how they make their money," Jean advised.

After a few more minutes of walking, we were back on Rue de Bonaparte. When we got back to 33 Rue de Bonaparte, there was a bouquet of carnations on the floor.

"That's not good," Jean said.

"Why's that?" Larisa asked.

"In France, the French say that carnations are the flowers of the dead. Come on Graham, we need to hurry," Jean replied.

"Fine by me," I said as I put the key in the lock and unlocked the top lock. Once I turned the key, it shattered in half, and half of it remained stuck in the keyhole. I shrugged and put the bloody thumbprint on the lock. The door opened with a creek. We were in!

There is only one way to avoid criticism. Do nothing, say nothing and be nothing —Aristotle

Chapter Six

We made our way through the flat and up the stairs. When we got up the stairs, we were greeted with a view that none of us were familiar with. The entire room was a lab, and one that we had never seen before, least not me back in medical school. I walked to the front of the first table.

"Uh guys, you're going to want to come here," I motioned.

They followed me.

"What is that?" Hannah asked.

"It looks like it's some broken down piece of a capstone. Oh my God," I said as I realized we had just seen it on Blur the night before.

Blur Slanders was talking about how a giant chunk was taken out of the Benben capstone and a giant piece was missing from the stone in the Kaaba as well. I think that's what we are looking at right here. I slowly made my way from station to station. There were beakers and cups with all forms of material in each of them. When we got to the final table, we saw two small balls of gold, the size of Ferraro Rochers.

"Guys, what do you think happened here?" Rosette asked.

"I think what we're looking at is a science experiment whereby one turns lead into gold," Jackson said.

"C'est impossible!" Jean shrieked.

"Supposedly it is. All the ancient people have tried to make this a reality through time. It's the ability to turn something useless into something useful. Quantum Physics and Alchemy have many overlaps between the studies, but unfortunately that's not my forte," Jackson said.

"It's not mine either," Larisa said.

One by one we looked at each other and realized that none of us knew much about it. I sat down on the one chair in the room. The legs were a bit wiggly. I stood up and kneeled down to try and fix it, when I found an envelope taped under the chair. I pulled it off and opened it. There was a letter.

Graham,

If you're reading this well done. I'm sorry about the Algol trickery before at the locks, but I had to make sure that only a master decoder would be able to figure it

out. My name is Jahzeel, but my name is irrelevant as nobody will ever be able to find me again. I'm what they call an 'agent of chaos.' I introduce a little bit of anarchy into the world, that is my purpose, and look at how the news has been going crazy over this. What you see in front of you is known as the Philosopher's Stone. Some call it the tincture, some call it materia prima, it doesn't matter. What you're seeing is the ability to turn 'lead' into 'gold'. This is the purest gold that has ever been found. If you've read your history, you know that the Annunaki came here from Nibiru in order to enslave men and make them mine for gold because their atmosphere desperately needed it. Our DNA was tinkered with, and consciousness exploded into humanity. All you have to do is look at the second chromosome in humans. It's 35% larger than the rest, and if you look at the middle of the horseshoe, it looks as if it has been fused together. This was no accident. This is also why there's such a vast difference in consciousness between humans and other creatures, though if you watch the news, you wouldn't know the difference. There are many people looking for me and my partner Syed, and many more will soon once this reaches critical mass. It is up to you to recreate our experiment and explode this new metal to the world. If you've been watching the MSM, you'd see that the Kaaba has been locked down and violence has taken the streets. Same in Cairo where the stone was carved. I can assure you that nobody was killed in the pursuit of these two stones, but I can't say that nobody was hurt along the way. Since the beginning of history, and probably dating back to the Annunaki, gold has been the safe haven against things such as inflation. It's a precious metal. Think back to your country's gold rush to the west. The San Francisco 49'ers are named after the gold rush of 1849. But why? Why is gold so important? It serves no purpose to keep us alive. It's shiny. But what's the point? The answer is, there is NO point to why gold is considered valuable. The amount of gold that has been on Earth has been greatly exaggerated as well. Fort Knox is empty. Supposedly there are three gold reserves in

Hawaii, but there's not much information on that. The point is that the financial system with fiat currency is about to collapse due to the inflation provided by the central banks throughout the world. This is not by accident. This is to introduce a one world currency. Oil used to be traded in Gold, until one of your presidents set a precedence that it would only be traded in United States Dollars. The dollars are useless. If you look on them it says 'for all debts, public and private,' it does not say it is backed by gold or silver. It's useless wads of cotton, and as far as gold goes, there's no practical reason why it's useful. That's why we set out to create a purer form of this. This is cleaner than 24k gold. Once enough of this gets out, it will invalidate all the rest of the gold in the world, thus sending the financial spheres, including those bastards who run the central banks, into a tailspin. It will be chaos. I know that you see things the way that I do. I've been reading your books. You see that the answer to every question on earth is money. The only way to be done with that is to make money and valuables obsolete. Much in the

same way that there is an enormous reserve of diamonds, and only a bit are let out every so often to keep the supply lower than the demand. The same with oil. There are many oil reserves which, if one was cracked and used, it could 'feed' the planet for a year. This entire system needs to collapse, unfortunately I've spent my life studying the ancient sciences in order to create this new material. My work is done. But you, with your platform, you can explode this onto the world and reset everything. Imagine how much better the World would be if the only things with value would be things that sustain us. I wish you luck Graham. Thank you for pursuing this. Much love to your wife, friends and child.

—Jahzeel

I stopped reading the letter and looked over at everyone. Everybody was quiet for a few until I spoke up.

"He's not wrong, you know," I said.

"Oh, come on Newsdon. You want to destroy society because this anarchist has a fetish for doing the impossible?" Rosette said.

"It's not that; thinking about it, it does make sense that we should at the very least try and duplicate it." Hannah replied.

"I agree, I would love to do that," Jackson said.

"Alright, then it's settled. We'll figure it out," Larisa said.

We looked at the stones, the beakers, the heaters, the liquids, and it occurred to us simultaneously that we didn't have a clue as to how to begin this.

"Guys, we're doing this all wrong," I said as I walked over to the wall and put my foot up on it.

"This is called alchemy, right?" Hannah asked.

Jackson nodded.

"Alright well, I happen to know an alchemist. I haven't talked to him in a while, but I follow his workings on Aquastream. We can all agree that none of us know what the hell we are doing, right?" Hannah asked.

We nodded.

"Alright, Jean, can we get this guy a ticket to Paris if he's willing to come?" Hannah asked him.

"Bien sure!" Jean replied.

"Alright, give me a minute guys, I'll go call him," Hannah replied as she whipped her cell phone out and walked down the stairs and across the hall.

We sat there for a minute until I yawned, and my foot slipped and went through a grate on the wall.

"Great job Graham," Larisa said.

"I know. FUCK. Wait, hold on guys, there's something in here," I said as I punched more of the wall out. "This is a false wall!" I shrieked.

I put my hands in the hole and pulled out what looked like a flashlight. I turned it on, and a blue light shined through it. There was a note wrapped around the base. I took it off and read it.

As above

I don't know what made me look at the ceiling with the flashlight, but there was hidden fluorescent writing on the ceiling.

"Guys, get the lights!" I shouted as Rosette motioned to Hannah to turn the lights off. Which she did.

I aimed the light at the ceiling, and we saw writings.

"Rosette, are you getting this?" I asked.

"Give me a sec," she replied.

Slowly we went over the ceiling and Rosette wrote down what was written on the ceiling. After she was done, we all stood up and Hannah turned the lights on. We looked at what was written, and none of us had anyway to make any kind of sense out of it. It might have been in a different language that doesn't even use our alphabet.

"It's done," Hannah said.

"Alright guys, I say we set up shop here for tonight instead of our hotel. Something tells me I don't want to leave this place alone," I said.

"Agreed," Jackson said.

We each packed into different rooms and went to bed. It was a long arduous day. If we only knew the kind of shit show that would happen tomorrow.

It can be revealed to one person in a moment, what has been denied to all of humanity for aeons.

—Kahlil Gibran

Chapter Seven

Half an hour ago

"Thank you for calling International, this is Dannick how may I help you?" Dannick said into the phone.

"Yes, I have some life-saving medicine that urgently needs to get to Canada," the voice on the other line said.

"OK sir. Where in Canada?" Dannick asked.

"Toronto, but it HAS to be there within 18 hours, or the medicine will no longer be valid," the voice said.

"What is your name?" Dannick asked.

"Tom from Atta Heal Therapeutics," he replied.

"Alright Tom, where are you located?" Dannick asked.

"I'm just outside Chicago," Tom replied.

"Alright then. I see here that you're on file. I've just emailed you a form I need you to fill out. Once I receive it back, I can get to work. Is this product ready now?" Dannick asked.

"It is," Tom replied.

"What is it exactly?" Dannick questioned.

"It's monoclonal antibodies that have been adjusted a bit," Tom replied.

"Alright, well I'm sending a driver over to you right now. Please show your ID to him when he picks up, he should be there very shortly," Dannick answered.

"Thank you so much. Please provide the tracking when you have it available," Tom requested.

"Don't worry. At the pickup, you'll be given what's called a House Air Waybill. This will have your tracking number on it," Dannick replied.

"I can't thank you enough," Tom said as he hung up the phone.

Dannick looked at his watch, his shift was almost over, but he had to figure this one out and route it. It was too late for anything to fly out of Chicago internationally, as those flights were earlier. Dannick put his phone on aux and took a walk outside to get some fresh air. He began to think about this one when one of his colleagues met him outside.

"How's it going Dannick?" His colleague asked him.

"Got a real banger here. Outside Chicago to Toronto within 18 hours," Dannick replied.

"That's a rough one. Got any ideas?" His colleague asked.

"So far nothing. I'm heading back in. It's good seeing you," Dannick replied.

Dannick walked back to his desk inside where he sat down and put his head in his hands. It was the policy of his company which was based in Queens, New York, to never turn any shipment down, but he felt like he backed himself into a wall with this one. Suddenly an email came through. It was the form requested as well as a commercial invoice and the permits necessary for customs. Dannick looked at the calendar on his wall and noticed the month and day. He had been a white glove logistics coordinator at this company for five years at this point, but he had never come across something like this. He opened the files and looked over the documents. Everything looked good. It wouldn't be a problem to clear customs, but how to get them there. Suddenly his phone rang. He looked down at it. It was Hannah from college. He hadn't heard from her in years. He let it go to voicemail as he had to figure this out before his shift ended in 20 minutes. He opened up the internet and pulled up a map of the United States and Canada. As he previously thought, there were no flights from Chicago to Toronto until late tomorrow morning, which with customs clearance and delivery from the local Toronto agent, would be too late. He considered something called a handcarry. This is where they pay someone to take the flight and bring the product with them, it would save time on customs and the bullshit handling of the crew to offload and onload the products from the plane. Unfortunately, there were no flights. He then considered getting a quote to charter a plane, but that would be too expensive. He would keep that on the backburner until there were no other options left. He stared at the map on his computer. These things always come out too blurry, he thought. He stood up and went to the back of his office where there was a larger clearer map on the wall. Suddenly he had an idea. He went to his computer and pulled up his program called OAG. This program allowed him to search any and all flights both domestic and international. It used to be a giant book, but technology progresses, and people were able to make it a computer program. He noticed that there was still a flight to Fargo left. Fargo was a four-hour drive to Winnipeg. He knew he had to think outside the box in these jobs, but this was beyond his purview. He would have to get approval as he didn't know if it had ever been done before. He walked into his boss's office and ran his idea by her. She absolutely loved it and gave him the green light; she would call the client back and give them a quote and explain the situation. Feeling good, Dannick went back to his desk and began working on it. After about 15 minutes, everything was set. He was going to send this package from Chicago to Fargo. Once in Fargo, the agent would recover it from the airline and give it to a HandCarrier who would take a train from Fargo to Winnipeg. Clear customs in Winnipeg, then jump on a flight to Toronto. ETA, 13 hours, including time zone changes. Dannick put the finishing touches on this and looked at his watch. His shift came to an end. He picked up his coat and put it on. He went into his boss's office and gave her a high five. She lauded him for a job well done and for thinking 'outside the box' which is what he was hired for. He walked outside and popped a mint before hopping on the subway. He gave Hannah a call back.

"Hi Hannah, it's Dannick. Is everything ok?" he asked.

"Hi Dannick. No things are fine, but we need your expertise, we are a bit lost," Hannah said.

"What do you mean?" Dannick queried.

"I'm with Graham and we're in the heart of Paris. We have something here that is beyond us that we can't understand, and we need your help. Can we fly you in?" Hannah asked.

Dannick sat for a moment. What the hell could he possibly be help with?

"Start from the beginning," Dannick pleaded.

"You know the missing capstone and the missing part of the stone at the Kaaba you've seen on the news?" Hannah asked.

Dannick's eyes grew wide. They were on another mission to figure some things out. This time they would need his help. But what for?

"What do you have for me Hannah?" Dannick asked.

"There are incantations on the ceiling of where we are. We can't make them out. We need your help with the alchemy of this room," Hannah said.

Dannick was in. Aside from being a top tier logistics coordinator for a premier courier company, he was a semi-expert in alchemy on the side. Combining that with his old friend, and he was in.

"Where do you want me to go?" Dannick asked.

"My friend Jean will fly you into Paris, and we'll come get you at the airport. Can you help us?" Hannah pleaded.

Dannick thought about it. Absolutely, he thought to himself.

"You're lucky it's the weekend and I already have off Monday anyway. I was going on a date tonight, but I think I can postpone it. I'm heading home to pack, and I'll jump on the red eye. Send me the ticket confirmation when you have it. I gotta go Han, I'm on the subway and about to lose signal," Dannick said.

"Ok, just make sure that you . . ." Hannah said as the call was dropped.

"Make sure what? Hello? Hello?" Dannick pleaded into the phone.

Dannick made his way back home to Astoria. He was going to take this girl he had been dating for a few weeks to the Beer Garden in Astoria, but he would have to cancel. If only he had heard what Hannah was saying on the other line before the call dropped. She would have told him not to tell anyone where he was going, including his date.

Tolerance will reach such a level that intelligent people will be banned from thinking so as not to offend the imbeciles —Dostoyevsky

Chapter Eight

We were waiting at CDG for Dannick to come in. I had met him once at a college party of Hannah's and they had remained in contact off and on since then. To be honest, I was surprised he would just hop a plane and come meet us. Rumor had it that he had a crush on Hannah, but never pursued it because we were always together. He was a nice guy like that. I wondered how he would be when meeting all of us, but mostly, if he would be able to help us out at all. After all, none of us were versed in this topic beyond what Blur Slanders and the conspiracy circuit had to say, which was mostly unflattering.

After another 45 minutes of waiting, a familiar face crept out of the door. Hannah opened her door and ran out and gave him a big hug. He looked pretty much like what I remembered of him. I got out of the car and walked up to him and shook his hand. I then took his suitcase and brought it to the back of the car and put it in the trunk.

"How are you, Graham?" Dannick asked.

"Oh, you know, just dragged into something I don't want to be a part of yet again," I replied.

"I heard. I'm not sure how much help I can be. Hannah wouldn't tell me what she needed from me other than it involves alchemy," Dannick advised.

"To be honest, I'm not so sure either, I just hope we didn't waste your time," I replied.

"And how are you Hannah girl?" He asked and smiled and gave her another hug.

"I'm good," she replied.

"So I hear you guys have a family now," Dannick replied.

"We have a 5-year-old boy, who gives me hell on earth, and an 8-year-old retired police K-9," I replied.

"Ouch. Got to be careful to never bring any pot in the house Graham," Dannick laughed.

Though him and Hannah haven't talked in a while, he must have caught my TV appearances from time to time as I shared bits and pieces of my life on occasion. We got in the car, and Jean drove us back to the house. He had Larisa stay at the house in the event the door got stuck with the key being in it and all. Jean dropped us off, parked around the corner, then ran back to us.

"OK, are you ready Dannick?" I asked.

"I guess so," he shrugged.

We went inside and up the stairs. We gave Dannick a few minutes to acclimate to his surroundings. He meticulously went from one table to the next, taking in everything. Finally, he got to the last table where he then picked up the two balls of gold. He studied them, then everything hit him all at once, and he dropped them on the table and stepped back.

"This can't be what I think it is," he said in shock.

"I'm afraid so," I replied.

"Since ancient times people have tried to translate lead into gold, or some other metal into gold. Countless geniuses, secret societies, people of prominence have. Where did you get all this?" He demanded.

"We were led here by a letter," Rosette said as she handed it over to him.

He read the letter that I had recently read out to everyone silently to himself. When he was done, he folded it twice and handed it back to Rosette.

"I'm going to have to explain this to all of you, aren't I?" he asked.

"Please. We have no idea what we're looking at here," Jackson said.

Dannick looked over at Jackson. "I had no idea in the car just how huge you are. You must be the physicist," Dannick questioned.

"You've read Graham's books?" Jackson asked.

"Of course I've read the books. They're really good books!" He exclaimed.

"Dannick, please. What are we looking at here?" Hannah asked.

"I suppose I have to initiate the 'unbegun,' " Dannick said.

"What do you mean by that?" Larisa asked.

"The unbegun. It's a New World Order term which is for people who haven't begun to understand these mystical sciences. Alright, let's start at the beginning. I'll have to give you the Robert Allen Bartlett condensed version of this, or we'll be here for weeks," he began. "The Greeks called Egypt Khem or Khemet. It's where we get the words Alchemy. When you attach the prefix Al from Arabic and Kehmia from Greek, you get alchemy. Most people nowadays have no idea what alchemy is; they think it's some ancient 'witchcraft' or 'potion making.' Some more intelligent people think that it is the beginnings of Chemistry. Incidentally 'chemistry' comes from Khem, or Al Khem. In 290 C.E., the Emperor Diocletian was scared that the influx of imitation gold produced by the Egyptian Art would destroy the Roman economy. Fearing also that it would allow someone to gather enough wealth to form an army which could move against Rome, he passed an edict calling for the destruction of all texts and materials dealing with the manufacture of gold and precious stones. Now, fast forward. Around 1310 Pope John XXII issued a decree prohibiting the practice of alchemy, and gold-making in particular, with huge fines against those who traded in alchemical gold and then in 1404, King Henry IV issued an act declaring gold-making a crime against the Crown," he advised.

"What's the big deal?" Hannah asked.

"This could disrupt the worlds currencies and what props up the universal economy, which is what they intend to do from this letter I just read," Dannick said.

"Go on," I replied.

"Right. Fast forward even farther. Isaac Newton considered himself to be more of an alchemist than a physicist or mathematician. His notes indicated that he believed he was very close to being able to turn metals into gold. Now, in the 1800's during the gold rush, the idea of turning lead into gold took a more metaphorical turn. The idea was that you take lead, turn them into bullets, sell them, get money, buy gold with the money. But the theory, the idea that you could turn something useless into something incredibly valuable has both a literal and a metaphorical use. Lead to gold is a metaphor for turning your lower self into your higher self, realizing all your chakras and becoming a God on earth. Verba Secretorum Hermetis. It is true, certain, and without falsehood, that whatever is below is like that which is above; and that which is above is like that which is below: to accomplish the one wonderful work. As all things are derived from the One Only Thing, by the will and by the word of the One Only One who created it in His mind. Its father is the Sun; its mother is the Moon. See, science is trying to find out how matter created life. This is where Jackson as you know, the God particle comes in. The thing that gives everything mass. However, alchemy states that life created matter, not the other way around," Dannick paused and grabbed a diet coke from the table, cracked it and took a sip. "This is where you come in Graham. It has been said that without knowledge of astrological tools and methods, the production of a true alchemical medicine is not possible. The same goes with old school Italians that make their own wine. You could only move wine when it's a white moon on the calendar. What mattered was when you transferred it. You need to make your so to speak potions at certain astronomical times." Dannick finished.

I stared bug eyed at him, then walked to the table and grabbed the blue light. I aimed it and traced over the ceiling. Dannicks eyes grew wide. "I wrote them all down," I said as I handed him another sheet of paper. I had transcribed everything from the ceiling onto paper. He read it over quickly, then put it in his pocket.

"Only by mental creation, can the All manifest the universe and still remain the All. For if a substance was used or acted upon, it would be separate and the All would not be All," Dannick said.

"Where's that from?" Jean asked.

"The Kybalion," Dannick replied.

"One of the biggest farces of our humanity is Descartes who said I think, therefor I am. Thinking does not confer existence. It may confer self-consciousness, but not existence. The correct way is the exact opposite. I am, therefor, I think. And with this, we are able to begin to figure out exactly what you guys have gotten yourself into," Dannick advised.

"What's with all these beakers and tubes?" Hannah asked.

"Glad you asked. There's something called Spagyric which comes from the Greek words meaning to separate and unite. That's what you're doing with these seven processes," Dannick advised.

"I don't follow. Seven processes?" Rosette asked.

"Right, I'm sorry. There are seven stages of Alchemy, that's what you see in front of you right now. They are, calcination, dissolution, separation, conjunction, fermentation, distillation, coagulation," he said.

"Sorts?" Jean asked.

"What?" Dannick asked back.

"Sorry, I mean, spells?" Jean asked again.

"In a sense. Words put together can cast spells. That's why it's called spelling," Dannick answered.

I had never thought of that before.

"What are these stages?" I asked.

"Calcination is when you subject something to enough intense heat and fire that it would produce white ashes called a 'salt'. Not to be confused with actual salt. Dissolution is when you transform a substance by immersing it in a liquid. The water then takes on the properties of the original substance, but in a purer more concentrated form. Separation is when you separate and filter the products of dissolution. Conjunction is when after the first three stages you have to combine the remaining elements. Then fermentation which occurs in two parts, putrefaction and spiritization, distillation is a level of further purification, finally coagulation wraps it all up. It is throughout history mostly been a metaphorical transformation of one's self, akin to Rosette's favorite Jungian archetypes. I can't believe that somebody cracked the code to literally transfer metals. Guys, we should burn this building to the ground and leave Paris immediately. This is too much power for someone to have," Dannick said.

"Dannick, we were BROUGHT into this lab via a complex code. Someone went through a lot of trouble to secure this away, send us on a wild goose chase to find it and that's with us having the letter to begin with. This information is already out there. If we don't do something here, someone else will," I replied.

"Alright, well at the very least let me look over that letter again," Dannick said.

"You have it in your pocket!" Jean said.

"Shit, you're right," Dannick said. He pulled out the piece of paper and looked it over. "Graham, where's Mercury at right now?"

"It's still in retrograde," I replied.

"For how long?" Dannick asked.

"For another two days," I said.

"Then we have to wait for two days to do anything," Dannick said.

"Why is that?" Rosette asked.

"Remember what I told you about the old school Italians and their wine? There're astrological implications to this. This probably shouldn't have been a problem, but you solved the riddle too early. They had assumed you'd be here a week or two later and wouldn't have to worry. We're going to have to camp out for 48 hours guys, I'm sorry," Dannick said.

"It is what it is," I said.

"But what about your work?" Hannah asked.

"I have a chance to turn lead into the purest gold that the world has ever seen before, I can afford a few sick days. Ora Et Labora!" Dannick replied laughing.

"What does that mean?" Hannah asked.

"Pray and work. We get the word laboratory from it," Dannick replied

"Alright well I'm exhausted, I'm going to go to bed," I replied and said goodnight to everybody.

As I crawled into bed and waited for Hannah to meet me, it occurred to me that I would never be able to think about esoteric sciences the same way again. Each time I think I have peace and quiet, someone comes in and skullfucks my brain with the deepest information possible.

The meaning of life is to find your gift, the purpose of life is to give it away —Picasso

Chapter Nine

4.5 days later

We all sat in one of the bedrooms. It had been four days since Dannick got here. We had to wait two days for Mercury to be out of Retrograde, and he had been working night and day for another two days. I looked at Hannah as she was on Larisa's computer.

"I don't know. 13 inches is a little small for me," she said.

I looked over at her.

"When did you become a size queen?" I asked.

She stared back at me, not saying anything for a moment.

"I need at least 16 inches," she replied.

"Did you ever watch Pawn Stars?" I asked her.

"Yeah why?" She asked back.

"Best I can do is six," I said laughing.

"Shut up Graham. I'm talking about a new laptop dumbass," she replied.

Everybody laughed.

"Hey Graham, speaking of which, do you know that physics tells us that in space, doggie style and reverse cowboy are the same thing," Jackson interjected.

"Excuse me?" I asked.

"Think about it," he replied.

I did for a moment and laughed.

"Oh yeah, I guess that is true," I said.

"Jackson, you packin?" Larisa asked and winked at Rosette. Rosette giggled.

"Wouldn't you like to know LGBT queen," he replied.

"I put the Queen in the Queen B of that part, and don't you forget it," Larisa said to him.

"You know, I understand lesbians, but gay men confuse me. I mean, doesn't sex hurt for them?" I asked.

"It's actually not that bad," Larisa replied.

We all looked at her.

"What do you mean? Jackson asked.

"They use poppers," she responded.

"What the hell are poppers?" Hannah asked.

"You sniff them. It's something called Amyl nitrate. It relaxes the muscles in the ass," she said candidly.

"Oh Solex, you are a naughty boy," Rosette said and laughed.

"You know that King James had three male lovers, right?" I asked.

"I mean, you know what they say. If you want to tell people the truth, make them laugh, otherwise they'll kill you. I believe that was Oscar Wilde," Jean replied.

"You know, I always wanted to be in a porn, but not as a performer. I wanted to be the husband or boyfriend that sits in the chair next to the bed with his head in his hands crying while someone is on the bed next to me plowing my wife," I said.

Everyone stopped and looked at me.

"Well, hey, it's easier to swing, once you got that ring, am I right Hannah?" Larisa asked.

Rosette giggled.

"Did you know that beer and vagina's have basically the same acidity levels?" Jackson asked.

"Well, I'm not using either anymore," I said.

"Oh, shut up Graham," Hannah said and laughed.

"Bro, you must have restless cock syndrome by now," Jackson said to me.

"I swear that you guys' birthstones must be crystal meth," Larisa said.

"Can we change the topic?" I asked.

"Sure," Rosette said.

"Hey Graham, do you know that Richard Dawkins said Astrology is rubbish, his words," Jackson said.

"Richard Dawkins is an idiot," I replied. "Jesus as 12 years old is referred to as the Most High. The Sun at the position at 12:00 noon is the original most high," I replied.

"Are you still doing your arena tour, or are you cancelling it because of everything going on?" Jean asked.

"No, I'm still doing it. It's just wild because I keep seeing similar faces everywhere I go, but for the life of me, I can't remember any of their names or what we've talked about," I replied.

"That's because of Dunbar's number," Rosette replied.

"What is that?" I asked.

"Dunbar's number. It's a suggested limit to the number of people who one can maintain stable social relationships. That number is 150," Rosette replied.

"It always goes back to psychology with you, doesn't it girl," Larisa said.

"If I had my life to live over again, I should devote myself to psychical parapsychological research rather than psychoanalysis. That was Freud, years ago. I'm starting to feel the same way, not going to lie," Rosette replied.

"Jackson, why did you bring up Richard Dawkins?" I asked.

"I didn't know if you knew he said that," he replied.

"It wasn't in my chart I had read last week," I said.

"You get your charts read?" Jackson asked.

"Everytime something major happens I do. Early on when I was starting out, I met this astrologer named Priscilla. She lives in Kentucky; we became online friends. She's the absolute best at chart reading that I've ever met; so I slide people over to her to get their charts done, and I still get mine done to this day from her," I said.

"Charts are just a play on the Barnum effect," Rosette said.

"What?" I asked.

"The Barnum effect. The psychological phenomenon that causes people to give high accuracy ratings to descriptions of their personality that supposedly are tailored just for them but are actually vague enough to apply to most people," she replied.

"I could see how some people could see it that way, but believe me it's not that way for me," I replied.

"I can't get over the fact that Jackson talked about something other than physics for once," Hannah said.

Jackson laughed. "Well, since you brought it up, there are no particles. In particle physics, everything originates in a toroidal field or energetic resonance. Matter is an illusion; matter is coalesced energy. Your body is a toroidal field of energy; therefore, you can interact with all things energetically." Jackson replied.

"The ancient sciences teach all of this buddy. Try something new on us," I said.

"Alright, well did you know that time is linear only in our dimension, it acts differently in higher dimensions. So, by all account when you shed your body and raise a dimension to the next level of existence, you could go back in time. What that means is that theoretically Graham, your next life after this one could be a girl from the Middle Ages, it doesn't necessarily have to be in the future. Physics says that the present also affects the past," Jackson thumped.

"Alright, this is making my head hurt," Larisa said. "Rosette, how do you lay under this giant horse and let him talk physics to you in bed. First, how do you even breathe under there?"

Rosette balled out in laughter, "To be honest girl, he doesn't talk about physics when we're in bed together messing around."

"So that's why our sex life is so good?" Jackson asked.

Everybody laughed.

"Well, I was born with a girth certificate. It'd be a shame to let it go to waste," Jackson said.

"A what?!" Jean asked.

We all laughed.

"So basically, you sleep with everybody?" Hannah asked.

"Before Rosette, basically. I was a philanthropenis," Jackson advised.

"Oh Lord," Rosette rolled her eyes.

"How much longer, I'm getting bored. When I get bored my mind races, and I start to get anxiety," Larisa said.

"Couldn't tell," Rosette said.

"Oh yeah, I go crazy in my head. Then I think everybody knows what I'm thinking, and I go even crazier. I can't sit still," Larisa said.

"When we're nervous we tend to overestimate how much other people notice our anxiety; this is called the 'illusion of transparency,' it's psychological. Don't worry, everyone has it," Rosette said.

"Well girl, you might be useful after all," Larisa said as she blew Rosette a kiss.

Rosette turned bright red.

"I swear there's something up with you two," I said to Rosette and Larisa.

"Maybe there is, maybe there's not. You wouldn't notice even if there was, you're too busy crying in your chair," Larisa said as everyone erupted.

"And you shall know the truth, and the truth shall make you free!" We heard Dannick shout from the other room.

"John 8:32. I'll go," I said.

I got up from the bed and walked into the other room. I was still in my pajamas, and it was incredibly warm in that room. I guess with all he was doing, there was a transfer of energy.

"You know Graham, in alchemy, gold is dominated by the Sun, makes sense, right? The most important thing in our universe that gives everything life and is the same color. Silver is dominated by the Moon, also that makes sense too. Copper by Venus, Iron by Mars, Tin by Jupiter, Mercury by Mercury, duh, and lead by Saturn. Now, as you've mentioned in your work before, Saturn used to be our 'second star.' In the ancient days it was a lot closer to us which is why people were able to see it. Like you say, the Jewish people's worship goes back to Saturnalia worship; it's why the women wore earRINGS, because they were told to listen to their God; it's also why you wear wedding RINGS, because you had to pledge your fidelity to your spouse, to your God. It's why when you graduate school you wear the black cube on your head. It's why judges wear black robes. It's why the Jews wear the tefillin and the black cube on their head; it's why the Muslims circle the Kaaba, a giant black cube. All Saturn. I was thinking about it, turning lead into gold. Lead being Saturn and Gold being the Sun. It's the evolution from the first Sun to the second Sun," Dannick said.

"I never considered that. So, what am I looking at here? Where are the black cubes?" I asked.

"Oh, I ended up using them both and combining them. Save you from hearing all the boring details of the seven stages, I've turned it into this," Dannick said as he picked up a Gold ball the size of a bocci ball and placed it in my hand.

"What is this?" I asked.

"Graham, that is a combination of the two stones. That is the purest gold that's ever been made on this planet," Dannick said.

"This is unbelievable," I replied. "Hey guys, get in here!"

Everyone stumbled their way into the main room.

"Is that what I think it is?" Rosette asked.

"It is," I replied as I handed it to her.

One by one each of them took turns handling this.

"I don't understand, these didn't come from lead," I asked Dannick.

"The lead part is a metaphor. The reason this works is because the Benben capstone and the Kaaba stone are not made from materials on this Earth. Theoretically it should work with anything extraterrestrial," Dannick finished.

"Like what?" I asked.

"Moon rocks," Jackson advised.

"Precisely," Dannick said.

"So, what are we going to do now?" Jean asked.

"Yeah, we have to do something don't we? We can't just keep this to ourselves," Hannah replied.

"Just let me think for a second," I said.

I paced around the room trying to think of the best way to do this. My Aquastream channel was being shadow banned at this point, so I wasn't able to reach as many people. I needed someone who could reach more. I also didn't want to use my mainstream TV contacts as they try and control the narrative. I sat down on the floor and pulled a CBD joint out of my pocket and lit it, took a deep inhale, then blew it out.

"Since when does Graham smoke pot?" Larisa asked.

"It's CBD. And if that's all he's doing, that's fine by my blood," Hannah replied.

I sat and smoked the pre-rolled joint. Halfway down it, I snubbed it on my shoe.

"I got it. I'll reach out to Rex," I replied.

"Who?" Jean asked.

"Rex Bear. He's got this channel called 'The Leak Project' and almost like 400,000 subscribers. I'm sure he would love to do this!" I yelped.

"Call him now, we have a five-hour time difference remember," Rosette said.

"On it," I said.

I flipped open my phone and gave him a buzz. We talked for a few minutes, and he said he would love to, just give him 20 minutes. I hung up the phone with him.

"Alright Larisa, can you set up the computer?" I asked her.

"On it. You're probably going to want to stream it from the bedroom so that people can't see where we are. You can see all the landmarks out the windows here," she replied.

"Excellent idea," I replied.

I took the ball back from Dannick after it made its way through everybody and walked into the bedroom. I had no idea just how viral this video was going to go and the things it would set in motion once it did.

You never change things by fighting the existing reality. To change something, build a new model that makes the existing model obsolete —Buckminster Fuller

If it's your calling, it will keep calling you
—Unknown

Chapter Ten

"Hey everybody, Rex Bear here, Leak Project. How the heck are ya? Today we have a very special guest that wants to break some news with us. Nanu nanu. So Graham, without further ado, how the heck are ya?" he asked.

"I'm great," I replied.

"So Graham, last time we spoke you were talking about some more of your decoding. Do you have anymore to share with us," Rex asked.

"Dan shall judge his people being one of the tribes of Israel. Dan shall be a serpent, biting the heels of the horse so the rider shall fall backwards. Genesis 49:17. The serpent is Ophiuchus, biting the heels of the horse, that's Sagittarius. Ophiuchus is between Scorpio and Sagittarius," I replied.

"Fascinating, so Graham, you have us all on edge. What do you have for us?" he asked.

"You're familiar with alchemy, right?" I asked.

"Somewhat. Why, what do you have?" he replied.

"Since the beginning of time, people have tried to turn 'lead into gold.' Now, for the alchemist this is a transmutation of the lower self becoming the higher self. Raising through the chakras, what have you. However, what if I told you that we were able to turn this," I said as I raised two small pieces of leftover material, "Into this," I said as I held up the giant ball of gold.

"Graham, do you mean to tell us that you turned lead into gold?" he asked.

"These two are remnants from the stone in the Kaaba, as well as the Benben stone. They were sent to an unknown location, and we followed a trail of clues to find them. I've been working with an alchemist to rec-reate the process that was done a little while ago and yes, we have the formula to turn lead into gold," I re-plied.

"This is incredible. So why share this with every-one? People are going to want to reduplicate it," Rex replied.

"The reason we are sharing this with the world, through you, first of all is because you're an awesome dude. Your heart is pure my friend. Secondly, the financial system has been screwed up in America since after Andrew Jackson's famous 'I killed the banks' last words quote. Chase bank manipulated silver, as silver to gold since the mid 1300's has always been a consistent ratio. Then in the early to mid-early 1900's when the federal reserve came into play, silver had been manipulated. JP Morgan Chase paid a 920-million-dollar settlement for manipulating the metals, this the time when Rockefeller was heading it. We are introducing a little anarchy to the system. This gold is so pure, that it should devalue all the rest of the gold in the world. If we can get people interested in alchemy while we're at it, that would be great," I replied.

"So why the Kaaba and the Benben?" Rex asked.

"Because those materials are not of this world. By theory, moon rocks, or King Tut's dagger, these should all be able to be used to make this new gold," I replied.

"We've got a question in the chat. Why are you showing up after 5 years of being quiet?" Rex asked.

"Well, I wouldn't say we've been quiet, I've been touring and talking about my work, but it's important to know that the financial institution as we know is not stable. Lincoln was about to print greenbacks which would have been money backed by actual silver. He was assassinated. Just about 100 years later, Kennedy signed executive order 11110 to print money backed by silver. He was assassinated. You're starting to see the pattern here? The dollar is a useless wad of currency, inflation keeps it blowing up, but we borrow from the Federal Reserve. Before 1913, people kept 100% of their paychecks. Since the Federal Reserve, inflation has shot through the roof. You borrow new money to pay back old money with interest. That's insane! Also, it's a pyramid scheme because you can never pay back enough of the money. Say I take out 1 trillion dollars. I take it out, with interest. I can never pay back the interest, unless we tax the people. We're basically up to anywhere from 25%-45% of income being taxed based on what you make, and it's useless paper. Read what a dollar bill used to say when it was backed by gold and what it says now. For all debts? What is that shit. Nah, dog. Also, why gold and silver? Who decided that these would be the markers for all eternity of value? Do they hold some substantive value? Can I eat it? Can I stay warm in it? What you're seeing now with cryptocurrencies, and why the elites hate them so much is they can't be attacked by central banks. Crypto is the way of the future. I talk about each Zodiac sign has a new religion, Aquarius being the sign of the man would be improving the man. Merging with machines, crypto etc. Pretty soon people will be trading with Bitcoin, Ethereum, and Shiba Inu. You're already starting to see countries accept them as forms of payments. There are Bitcoin ATMs popping up all over the place. This is why we're breaking this to the world and when I get off this podcast, I will send you the formula," I finished.

"Well Graham, aren't you worried that people are going to raid places that have these 'out of this world' stones?" Rex asked.

"I'm counting on it. You have to understand Rex, the system is irreparably broken. Inflation makes the dollar more useless every day. The world is in debt to itself by hundreds of trillions of dollars, and the only ones who end up on top are the bankers. There's a story in the Bible about Jesus flipping over the money changers tables. Money has been the root of all evil since the beginning of time. We need to make it so that a new valued currency comes out. This will force their hand," I thumped.

"Well, it all sounds great Graham. I hope you succeed with this. I can get behind this, maybe we can do another show once everything collapses? Nanu nanu," Rex said.

"You can count on it," I repeated.

"Thanks for the brief but informative chat old friend. Good luck. For those of you listening, get ready for the storm," Rex said as we signed off.

I closed the laptop and went back into the other room with my friends.

"Dannick, I need that 'recipe' list of how you did what you did," I said.

"Sure, here you go," he replied as he handed me a piece of paper. I took my cell phone out and snapped a picture of it then texted it over to Rex. In about 24-48 hours all hell will break loose.

When one loses the deep intimate relationship with nature, then temples, mosques and churches become important —Jiddu Krishnamurti

Chapter Eleven

36 hours later

Hawk Cublass sat in a room full of very uneasy men. It was all over the news and nobody could escape it. People were raiding the Space Center Houston's Lunar Vault and taking all the moon rocks. All around the world, people were stealing pieces of meteorites that were on display in museums. The Kaaba had been completely run over and the stone no longer existed there. Neither did the Benben stone. Those were the first to go. Now thanks to this prick's instructional video, people were making their own level of top tier gold and trying to sell it for money. Because it had come from such rare material, it would sell for enormous money. The stock market took a dive as people were pulling all their money out, being terrified of what was happening. The gold and silver indexes were incredibly low. The Fed had their foot on the pedal as far as printing money goes. The quantitative easing would be forever, Hawk thought.

"Gentlemen, please take a seat and let's get started," Hawk said.

"What's the use? The entire system is collapsing. Money is becoming worthless," one man said.

"Money has always been worthless, it's what we had in reserve in the gold and silver and precious jewels that was what kept it afloat. We have begun the process of transferring this society's money into Bitcoin and Ethereum," Hawk said.

"Crypto?!" One man shouted.

"It's the wave of the future," Hawk replied. "Also, what choice do we have?"

Hawk looked out at the group of 200 people. Mostly heads of banks and royalty. This was not what they intended on using the Quantified World Ecumenical Energy Federation for when they started it up a few years back, yet here they were.

"Gentlemen, it seems this is one thing that we cannot get our way out of. Many of us are taking billions in losses by the week, and soon will be by the day. We knew this was a house of cards that would collapse once it was exposed. Are you so shocked that it happened in our lifetime?" Hawk asked.

The room was dead silent.

"I say that if we can't have it, then nobody can. They will all have nothing, and they will be happy! Then, they will all perish. It seems the only answer to me is to use the great device," Hawk said.

"The device? You can't be serious? No, it's too soon. We just entered Aquarius," one man said.

"Can you think of something else that we could do? Do you want to go out there and live amongst, THEM!" Hawk shrieked as he pointed outside.

"No, this can't be. There are other options. What about the smallpox hysteria being jolted up right now?" another man asked.

"Temporary situation. The reality is that we have the city under the Sphinx, the city in the center of Antarctica, even the lost golden city 'Aten' was discovered. It's not just there. We have the city under Denver just itching to be filled. For the last 24 hours I've had planes full of supplies flown to all these locations to stock up. Most of them are fully functioning cities with their own ecosystems. If we can't live in luxury, then maybe nobody should. But at least, we'll all still be fine," Hawk replied.

"Is this the right course of action?" one man in the front asked.

Hawk turned on the TV.

For the last two days people have raided all places that have extraterrestrial

material. Labs have been bought up across the World where people are following the plans that were released from Rex Bears 'The Leak Project.' Rough estimates indicate that about 50lbs of extraterrestrial pure gold has been produced sending the markets into a frenzy. Protests have been jumping out in front of nearly every central bank in the World. Some, such as in America for example have been burned to the ground. Hundreds of arrests have been made. With no way to print money, Congress has halted the passing of all bills across the floor. People are trading in their old gold in record numbers, and pawn shops are thrilled to take them in at a discounted price. Some feel that this will pass. This has been Jennifer Polizzi, signing off.

"Do you see another way?" Hawk asked.

The Quantified World Ecumenical Energy Federation deliberated for about an hour or so. Each row set up at a table and they voted. The votes were then tabulated. In an overwhelming majority, they had voted to move forward with Hawk's plan.

"Gentlemen, in a few hours you will all be given slips of paper that tells you where you will go, and what section you will live in. I've been there. You will find that it is incredibly spacious and comfortable," Hawk said.

"What about everybody else?" another man asked.

"The 'device' will take care of that. It's literally time for us to rebuild civilization. Once the device is ready, it will set off a chain of events that will blanket the world," he said.

"What if it doesn't take everybody out? What about those that survive?" a man in the front asked.

Hawk looked at the man, he seemed a bit shaken.

"Brother, do not worry. Every 700,000 years there is an eruption that causes a mass wipeout. If you look at the timeline, we are right on the cusp of it. It will be seen as such. Truth is, we as a society have done nothing to prevent this event from happening, though we've known about it for many years. I think you'll find things will work out just fine, praise Algol!" Hawk said.

"Praise Algol," the people repeated.

Doreulla Laumilgan, the man in the front nodded his head and smiled. He tried to play it off like he was cool, but he was vehemently against what was being done. He knew there was only one person who would be able to expose such a plot. If he went public with this, the media machine would have just discredited him, and he probably would have ended up suicidal. He knew he didn't want that to happen, though he did think humanity was at the end of its ropes. No, this needed careful planning. He couldn't even risk telling any of his counterparts, because he didn't know where they all sat. This, he thought was the 'last call' for a dying society. Since the beginning of time, things have always had value and a trade system had been in place. Graham Newsdon had thrown a wrench in the thousands year old system. Unfortunately, he knew that Graham was the only person he could trust at this point, even though it might get him brutally killed in the future, despite all the complications going on in his life at the moment.

You will live to see man-made horrors beyond your comprehension —Tesla

Chapter Twelve

We were talking and laughing with one another, making jokes in the flat on Rue de Bonaparte where we made the magic happen. Everyone was in high spirits, and we were just having the time of our lives when my phone started to ring. I looked down. Weird. I didn't recognize this number and it was calling from Whats App. I picked up the phone.

"Hello Graham, this is Graham Newsdon, right?" the voice asked.

"Who is this?" I asked.

"I don't have a lot of time. Turn on the news right now," the voice said.

I went back into the room with everyone. I put my finger to my lip telling them to be quiet. I turned on the TV. Flipped to the news channel. There was nothing going on but talking about some protest.

"I don't see anything here guy," I replied into the phone.

"Not the French news Graham, the American one," the voice replied.

I changed the channel.

At this moment there are too many to count. Earthquakes have devastated San Francisco, Illinois, Indiana, Missouri, Arkansas, Kentucky, Tennessee, Oklahoma and Mississippi. This has originated from the New Madrid fault system that was shattered with an earthquake this morning. As of right now the national guard and FEMA have been dispatched to help search for survivors. The dead are rumored to be in the tens if not hundreds of thousands. Is this God being angry with us? Is this the end of times that were predicted in the Holy Bible. It sure seems that way. Major CEO's and higher ups are stepping down from their companies and moving out of the United States. When we have more, we will be back. Until then, this is Jennifer Polizzi now with AquaNews, signing off.

I turned the TV off in shock. Everybody in the room looked pale as a ghost.

"You see that, Graham? Put me on speakerphone with your friends," the voice said.

I did. "Who are you?" I asked.

"Who I am is not important, however my name is Doreulla Laumilgan. Graham, what you and your friends have done has set off a chain reaction that I fear I cannot stop in my condition," the man said as he started violently coughing into the phone. After a moment or two, he collected himself and stopped.

"I don't understand, what do you want from me?" I asked.

"You need to put an end to this. These earthquakes were not natural. They were caused by a machine. A very old machine that we've had the blueprints for over a hundred and twenty years. The elites have an end plan," Doreulla Laumilgan said.

"And what would that be?" I asked.

"To destroy the world. To fulfill the prophecy of the Georgia Guidestones rule #1. Only this time, they do not want to keep the world population to 500 million. They want to destroy everybody but themselves," Doreulla Laumilgan said.

"How do you know that?" I asked.

"Because Graham, I am one of them," Doreulla Laumilgan replied.

"What do you need from me?" I asked as I scanned the room to all the disbelieving faces.

"I need you to come home and meet me. I will meet you at the Frost Ice Bar on State Street. I have something that will help you. I will be there in 36 hours exactly and wait exactly 45 minutes. If you're not there, you'll never hear from me again," Doreulla Laumilgan said as he hung up the phone.

I stared at the blank phone in my hand for a minute while I collected my thoughts.

"Jean, get the plane ready, we've got to get the hell out of here," I said.

"On it," Jean said as he flipped his phone and went into the other room.

I sat down on the chair. Hundreds of thousands? The last time we had heard of a loss similar to this was that suicidal flu vaccine, but even that didn't touch these numbers. They haven't hit the East Coast yet, so that appears to be a good sign. We talked about this for a few minutes and then went in the other room to pack. Within an hour we were on our way to the airport. I gave the flat one last lookover to make sure we didn't leave anything. We didn't. There was no sign of any of us here. I went up to the table and took a ball of gold that was made and put it in my pocket. It's probably a good thing not to leave this behind. We made our way into the cold night air and into the taxi's. After about an hour due to traffic, we were at the airport and boarding the plane. I looked around at everybody. The cab driver and the people working at the airport, working, like nothing was happening in the World. This news must not have hit here yet. It would be a matter of time until this hit International. After a short wait, we were wheels up and in the air. We had discussed as a group and decided that Jackson and I would go alone to meet this man. I needed some muscle there incase this was going to be an ambush. Not that Jackson and I haven't been tortured together before. I closed my eyes and tried to get some sleep.

I awoke in a cold sweat. I had a dream that the entire country was swallowed into a big fiery hole in the ground and people were screaming to get out. I've never had dreams like this before, but it felt so real. I didn't have any idea if this was the reality that awaited us once we touched down in Boston. Would the device be used in the East Coast? Time was not our friend.

If nobody hates you, you're doing something wrong
—Dr. House

Chapter Thirteen

1 hour ago

"Gentlemen, thank you for meeting on such short notice. I notice that many of our members couldn't make it as they were busy stepping down from their companies and spinning PR for it, so thank you for those that are able to be here," Hawk said.

"What is the meaning of this meeting?" one man asked.

"Fellows, have you seen the news?" Hawk asked.

They shook their heads.

"You're right, it's not on it yet. That's fine. We have tested the devices. One in San Francisco and one on a fault line. Fellows, the device works, and it works better than we could have ever imagined. Early reports have no idea, but by our estimates, everything is in order. Half a million people dead so far," Hawk said.

"What is the next step?" one man asked.

"We're going to set this last device at a place where once it starts working, will set off a chain of reaction that will take out the entire United States," Hawk said.

"Where is that going to be?" another man asked.

"I can't share that yet," Hawk said.

"What if they find the device?" Another man questioned.

"What if they do? The beautiful thing about the device is the immediate area around the device, the land gets ripped apart by it. It falls into the fire below. Even if, and this is a big if, even if they are able to locate it, what do you think they'll think it is? It's not big, it's destroyed, and nobody has seen something like it in the last 100 years. Brothers, we are in the clear!" Hawk triumphed.

"Well, what about Graham Newsdon?" the first man asked.

Hawk's demeanor turned dark.

"Graham Newsdon is not a problem. The entire United States will be turned to ash within 48 hours. Brothers, the truth is that this is what we've been waiting for. We've been spending too much money on disinformation in the news, social media, medicines, foods, products. Slowly poisoning everyone, fluoridating the shit out of them. Lowering the population and for what? Trillions of dollars wasted and it's only NOW that people are not reproducing at replacement rates in the United States. All Graham Newsdon and his dipshit friends have done was accelerate the timeline.

Remember, we are in the Age of Aquarius right now. Aquarius is the sign of the man, and we are evolving as such. We were worried about whether or not we'd be able to spread a new holy book for people to fight over. Technology with social media, cameras everywhere has made it impossible for the new age religion to grow 'organically,' " Hawk laughed when he said organically, because he knew that every religion was spread through warring. Warring is good for profits, but any new religion that would come up would be shut down before it got too powerful. Also, Graham had exposed the Church for creating Islam, for hiding the Astrology meanings of the Bible, and pretty much shut down every single opportunity they had. He'd be out celebrating with his friends, not knowing he had about 46 hours to live.

"Gentlemen, I think we should celebrate. By now, each of you has received your address and directions for your new home. We have already been open armed received by the civilization under Antarctica. This is a great day for us, so let's party," Hawk said as he nodded to the doorman, who opened the door as strippers, alcohol, and food was being wheeled in.

The men partied for a few hours before Hawk defected to his room. He lay down in bed, a bit drunk and smiled. Little did he know, one of the members of the Quantified World Ecumenical Energy Federation, still partying was missing four members. There was one member that hasn't resigned his post from the Board of Directors at his company, and he was on his way to help Graham out.

Obviously astrology has much to offer psychology, but what the latter can offer its elder sister is less evident —Carl Jung

Chapter Fourteen

We were mid Atlantic in our flight when I turned Blur on.

I'm telling you people something is going on with the Quantified World Ecumenical Energy Federation. All the people there but FOUR have stepped down from their positions in companies around the world. I don't think the Earthquakes are the end of it. Also the Mayborough meteorite has been dismantled. People are running out of places that carry extraterrestrial stones.

I closed my computer and turned to Larisa.

"So how often does Jean visit your breastaurant?" I asked.

She was thrown completely off guard.

"About 15 minutes ago in the bathroom. He wanted to join the mile high club and I figured why not. How about you? Do you find time with a kid at home to pull a Hannah?" she asked.

"Ha! Try having a kid. I'd be lucky to get 5 minutes alone in the bathroom. But I will tell you this. I always thank all the porn stars who have always been there for me when I needed them the moist," I said.

Rosette giggled.

"Well, you do know that Hitler invented the blow-up doll. He gave them to Nazis so they could stop spreading Syphillis," Rosette injected.

"Alright that's just gross. So Larisa, why didn't you ever go to work for the FBI?" I asked as she was messing around on her computer.

"The FBI struggles to hire hackers because applicants must not have used marijuana in the last 3 years," she said.

"Really? Well, that's just stupid and doesn't make sense. Blood tests only go back a month and hair tests only go back six months, so I have no idea how they would even know," I responded.

"I have no idea, but honestly, I make way more money not working for the man," Larisa said.

"I have Deja Reve right now," Jean said as he made his way from the back of the plane.

"Well now, I was worried that the plane was starting to feel a little heavy, but since you dumped your kids off at the pool, I think we're going to be ok now," I replied.

'Quoi?" Jean asked, completely missing the joke.

"Never mind, I said.

"So what are you doing on the computer?" I asked Larisa.

"Well, just checked my email and I got my pirate certificate," she replied.

"What is a pirate certificate?" Jackson asked.

"MIT awards pirate certificates for students who take archery, pistol shooting, sailing and fencing," Larisa replied.

"So, you're like an official pirate? How sexy," Jean said.

"What else you got going on there?" I asked Larisa.

"I just hacked into the database for Daniel's Hosting and trying to see if there's any chatter about what Blur just talked about. Maybe we can find information about Doreulla Laumilgan before you meet him," Larisa said.

"What's Daniel's Hosting?" Hannah asked.

"It's the largest free web hosting for the dark web. There's some sick shit down here by the way, I wouldn't suggest going to it on an empty stomach," Larisa said.

"I'm starting to feel a little run down anyway," I replied.

"Oh great, he's getting a cold. You know, it was only when I gave birth, that I finally understood what a man cold was all about," Hannah replied.

Larisa laughed.

"Well, you know that among the Huichol Indians, the father would sit above his wife in labor with a rope tied around his balls. When she felt a contraction, she would tug on the rope so that he would experience the pain which would bring new life," Hannah replied.

"Yeah no, not going to happen!" Jackson replied.

"So, you have to go to the Frost Ice Bar, in late fall, in Boston, while you might be coming down with a cold. Why did he pick that place? I'm not thrilled about this," Hannah said.

"It's fine, if it gets really cold, I can just slide into Jacksons coat with him, and he'll keep me warm," I replied.

"Hetero life mates for life bro!" Jackson replied.

"At least it's not a brewery," Rosette said.

"Why's that?" Jackson asked.

"Breweries are full of people with cenosillicaphobia," she replied.

"And that is?" I asked.

"Fear of an empty beer glass. Also, breweries are just bars for people who can't fight," she finished.

Jackson and I looked at each other then burst out laughing. She was right.

"Give me a hug girl," I said as I went over and hugged her.

"You know that you never actually touch anything, right? Your atoms electrons repel objects when they are 10-8 meters away from you, but you can feel the force of resistance. Technically, you are actually hovering off the ground right now," Jackson said.

"I don't know how you keep sliding physics into my DM's bro, but way to kill the moment," I replied.

"First we have molecules, then atoms, then protons, electrons, neutrons, then quarks, then strings. There's probably a lot of things in between quarks and strings; however, until we have the Planck microscope, we'll never know," he finished.

"Well, at least we know that you won't go to hell, because you'll bore Satan to death," Rosette replied.

"Don't bring up Satan, we all know what that truly is," I replied. "Did you know that on Voltaire's death bed when he was asked to renounce Satan he said 'now now my good man, this is no time for making enemies.' "

"Speaking of making enemies, remember how I told you about that Jewish guy I dated back in the day. So his family was very religious, and he had slept over at my house the night before. In the morning his dad came to pick him up and had to use the bathroom, but I was in the middle of frying up the juiciest bacon you could ever imagine. When I saw him come to the door, I panicked not knowing what to do so I grabbed the frying pan and shoved it in the fridge and turned the fan on," Rosette said.

We laughed.

"You know, bacon doesn't kill Jews, right? This isn't like garlic and vampires," I replied.

"I was 16," she responded.

Everyone this is your pilot, we should be approaching Boston within the next 20 minutes or so, please get ready

"Alright guys, everybody back to your seats," I said.

"I haven't heard any new astrology from you this ride. Are you feeling ok?" Jackson asked.

"Yeah, I'm just not feeling too hot. I'm going to pop an airborne and pound an orange juice," I said.

"Sorry to hear that," Jackson said.

"Hey guys, I got something," Larisa said.

"What you got girl?" I asked.

"Blur was right; there were four people that didn't step down yet and none of them are named Doreulla Laumilgan. I'm sending you their info right now to your phones," she replied.

"Good, we'll have a look at it on the way back to our house," I said as I popped some zinc, vitamin C, a multivitamin and washed it down with orange juice. We were 10 minutes out from landing. We had no idea what to expect when we got to the Frost bar, but from the way Doreulla Laumilgan was speaking to us, it couldn't be good.

A physician without a thorough knowledge of Astrology has no right to call himself a physician

— Hippocrates

Chapter Fifteen

We landed in Boston and Jackson and I took an uber to the Frost Bar. I hadn't been to a bar in forever since I quit drinking years ago. It's funny. I used to get anxiety and depression so I'd drink in order to level me out and it would make me feel better for a little bit, until the next day when I felt worse than before, repeat cycle. However, it turned out that the drinking was the problem all along. Everyday I felt amazing, I literally had no use for alcohol anymore. We walked to the front door and the bouncer checked our ID's. When the bouncer saw my name he smiled and rolled up his arm to show a rabbit going down a hole. I had yet to run into someone with an Into the Rabbit Hole tattoo, yet here I was. He let us right in. We walked around looking for someone who might be Doreulla. We saw a man sitting along, furiously typing on his computer. When he looked up and noticed us, he smiled. He closed the laptop and stood up and reached out.

"An invisible thread connects those who are destined to meet, regardless of time, place, and circumstance. The thread may stretch or tangle. But it will never break. It is so nice to meet you Graham," Doreulla Laumilgan said as he reached his hand across to mine.

"What is it we can do for you?" I asked.

The old man started coughing into his hand, then slumped down in the ice chair and started coughing even more. I noticed that his eyes were yellow.

"Hold on a second Doreulla, I said as I grabbed my mini flashlight on my keychain. I went up to him and opened his eyes and flashed it deep into them. His eyes were yellow, and he had golden rings around his corneas.

"How long have you had Wilson's disease?" I asked him.

The man smiled. "Can't take the doctor out of you, can they?" he answered.

"Judging by your signs, I'd say you have three to six months left," I replied. "But you knew that already, didn't you?"

The man nodded. "I've lived a full life with many regrets. You don't get to my power level without breaking a few eggs. As you get older and death knocks, you start thinking about your afterlife. If afterlife is Karma for life on Earth, sometimes you try your hardest to make some changes. My name is not Doreulla Laumilgan by the way. This is not my real voice, and this is not my real face either. I can't risk you knowing who I am," he replied.

"Relax I know who you are Kernal Agleam," I replied.

The man's jaw dropped, or his mask's jaw dropped. I have no idea.

"How?" he asked.

"Blur Slanders said there were four people that haven't stepped down from their post yet. We looked at the list. Your voice may have changed, but you're the only one of the four with a Swedish accent," I replied.

The old man looked dejected. "Look guys, I have no idea who's tracking me," he replied.

"Did you have to pick a frozen ice bar in Boston at the end of the fall for this meet?" I asked.

"This would be the last place anybody would look for you, this is precisely the reason I selected this place," the man said. "As of right now, nobody knows that you know anything, but we don't have very long," the man said as he started coughing into his hand again and slumped back down in his chair.

"I'll get you a glass of water," Jackson said as he turned around.

"Wait," the man said, but Jackson had already left. The old man turned back around at me and smiled. "You're incredibly bright Graham. Your friends are monumental in helping you out, but this one you're going to have to put it all together very quickly. I unfortunately do not have all the answers you're looking for, but I have some. There were some things that weren't shared with us in the room. Hawk made sure of it. But here, you're going to need this," the man said as he opened his mouth, took out his dentures, and put them in a plastic bag and handed them to me.

"What the hell am I going to do with your teeth old man?" I asked.

"Relax," he said as he put a new set of dentures in, the teeth looked different than the others. "You'll figure it out."

Jackson came back with the water and looked at the teeth in my hand.

"I leave you alone for 5 minutes and you rob the old man? Or did you just knock him out?" Jackson asked.

"Chill, he gave them to me. He said the answer's in there," I replied.

"Just one of the answers. Now listen carefully. I can't write this down for fear that someone will see it so I'm going to tell you this just once and then leave. This is all that I know incidentally. In the excommunicated land stands Santa Maria. There, a Zodiac stands tall guarding the entrance. Within it you'll find the Sun beneath the Sun. Follow the trail and it will point to an old-world gold. The secret is underneath it," Kernal replied.

"What is the secret?" I asked.

"It's the location of the device," Kernal said.

"What device?" Jackson asked.

"The device that is causing all the earthquakes around the world. The first two were nothing compared to what's coming. Now, excuse me gentlemen, I have to go," the old man stood up and I handed him his cane. He walked up to us and shook our hands and wished us luck. He then sauntered his way out of the bar, with Jackson and I looking at each other.

"Hide the teeth in your pocket bro," Jackson said.

I had forgotten I was even holding them. I stashed them in my pocket, and we walked out of the bar and into a waiting taxi. In the car ride home, I was thinking to myself. Is it the dental imprints, the DNA from the saliva? What could this possibly be. Little did we know that the countdown to the end of civilization was already ticking down.

*Things are not getting worse, they are getting un-
covered. We must hold each other tight and continue to
pull back the veil —Adrienne Maree Brown*

Chapter Sixteen

We got back to my house. We didn't really know what
to make of our encounter earlier. How did we know he
was on our side? How did we know he wasn't setting us
up so that the elites could finally take me out? We had
to go on best available info at the time, and we decided
to trust him. I walked into the kitchen and grabbed a diet
coke from the fridge.

"Alright guys, so what exactly are we waiting for?"
I asked.

"We have no idea what you're talking about. You
literally just got home," Rosette said.

"Crap, right," I said as I took a huge gulp of the soda.

"We met one of the missing four at the bar," Jackson
began, "he gave us these," he finished as he dropped the
dentures in a bag on the table.

"What in the hell is that?" Larisa asked.

"They look like teeth to me," Jean said.

Larisa shot him a look and rolled her eyes. "I know they're teeth Jean, Jesus. What are we supposed to do with them?" she asked.

I put on a pair of latex gloves and carefully took them out of the bag. I held them up to the ceiling. I opened them and examined the teeth and the mouth.

"Hey riss, do you think you could get dental prints off this?" I asked.

"Let me get my scanner and let me see if my back door is still operational to do a search," she replied.

I waited a moment until she brought the scanner. I placed the teeth on it, and the scanner did its job. A picture showed up on her computer. After slight editing, she was able to isolate the teeth.

"I'm running them right now," Larisa said.

We talked for a few minutes while her computer did her thing until we heard a beep. All at once we stopped talking.

"Guys, we have an issue here," Larisa said.

"What would that be? Dannick asked.

"These teeth aren't from one of the four. The print matches a Hawk Cublass," she expounded.

"You've got to be kidding me?" I emphasized.

"What? Do you know him?" Larisa asked.

"He's the guy that's been all over social media. He's the one that's famous for saying 'They will have nothing, and they will be happy,' " I replied.

"Well, what does that give us exactly?" Hannah asked.

"What it does, is tell us who we're after," I replied.

"Great. Unfortunately, nobody has seen him since all those CEO's stepped down. What are we supposed to do? Search the globe for him?" Jackson asked.

"We do have a plane," Jean interjected.

"And where would that plane be heading off to first? No, you know what? I'm sick of this shit. Jean, can you book us a plane to Cabo San Lucas. I say we all take a vacation there," I said as I picked the teeth up. "We can bring Mr. Hawk Cublass with us," I finished.

"Now you're just being ridiculous," Dannick said.

"Maybe, but I'm sick of these riddles and these games. Doreulla Laumilgan, no wait, Kernal, Hawk, shit I don't know, told us that in the excommunicated land stands Santa Maria. There a Zodiac stands tall. Within it, you'll find the Sun beneath the Sun and it points to an old-world gold. The secret lies beneath it," I finished.

"I have no idea what any of that means," Dannick advised.

"You don't," I began, "because none of us do. This whole thing is a test of my fucking patience," I said. As I lifted my hand to emphasize patience, I dropped the teeth. I tried to catch it and ended up fumbling it and caught it by its two front teeth where they slightly detached.

"Look, you broke the thing, tsk tsk," Jean said.

I looked closer at it and wiggled the front teeth a little more. Suddenly the two front teeth detached and revealed it to be a flash drive. My eyes grew wide as I took it and looked at it in the light of the chandelier.

"You've got to be kidding me Newsdon," Rosette said.

"Larisa!" I shouted.

"She put her hand out and I placed the teeth flash drive into the computer and started working furiously at it.

"Of course there's a failsafe password on this thing," Larisa said.

"You mean one guess, and if nothing, it deletes?" I asked.

"Exactly Graham," she replied.

I put my hand on my beard and started stroking it calmly. Everything is connected I kept being told from adventure to adventure. What could this be?

"Do you know how many letters it is?" I asked.

"Negative," Larisa replied.

"Ok then, well what do we know," Jackson asked as he dropped down and started doing pushups.

"Is this the time or the place meatball?" I asked.

"It helps me think, gets the blood rushing to my brain," Jackson replied.

"What about what he told us. Usually, people hand us pieces of paper with riddles on them, but he was very clear that he didn't know who was around and couldn't chance getting caught, so he told us verbally. I looked down and Jackson was already 50 pushups in with no sign of slowing down.

"In the excommunicated land stands Santa Maria. So, Mary basically. But what's the excommunicated land. Usually, people are excommunicated not land.

Rosette picked up her laptop that she had left at our house by accident a few nights ago and started Duck Duck Going things.

"The Sun beneath the Sun, what if that's talking about Jesus?" Hannah asked.

I turned to her. "You mean astrology again?" I asked.

"He said the Zodiac stands tall. If this is Jesus beneath Jesus, the SUN of God, then that would mean that this would have to be a Church, no?" Hannah replied.

"Rose girl, can you find an excommunicated Church? Did the Vatican excommunicate any Churches?" I asked.

"On it, give me a few minutes," she replied.

"Dannick, what do you think?" Jackson asked as he stood up.

"I don't know guys; this kind of stuff is way outside my purview. I'm just the alchemist remember," he replied.

"I got something," Rosette said.

"What is it?" I asked.

"In the 13th century, the entire village of Trasmoz in Spain was excommunicated for witchcraft, and in 1511 Pope Julius II ordered the village to be cursed. Neither of them was ever lifted. The town in June awards a witch of the year during the Feria de Brujeria festival," she replied.

"That has to be it. Larisa try Trasmoz," I replied.

"Are you sure Graham, we only got one shot at this," she retorted.

I thought back to our first escapade when I was walking outside of Senna Ore, and I figured out that the password was Aquarius. I hadn't thought back to that in so long. For some reason, I was just as sure of this one as I was for that one.

"Just do it," I said as I put my hands up in praying motion and held them to my lips. Then I realized that my gloves were still on, and I was wiping the dentures saliva all over my mouth. I started spitting on the floor, took the gloves off and launched them across the room.

"The password worked, we're in," Rosette said.

"Perfect," I replied.

Gold is the money of kings, silver is the money of gentlemen; barter is the money of peasants; debt is the money of slaves —Norm Franz

Chapter Seventeen

I turned on Blur to see what else was going on.

The Fukang meteorite was stolen. Nobody is reporting on this, but it has been rumored that this 2000-year-old plus meteorite that was formed when our solar system was first created has created 1983 pounds of the purest gold of them all. In other news, the total death count from the Earthquakes in the United States has toppled over 2 million people and the globalists that run things are nowhere to be found.

I turned the TV off.

"Alright guys, so where are we?" Dannick asked.

"So, there's a few encrypted files here and one live link. I'm working on the decryption right now, but it can take a little while as I have to find the primer to unlock it," Larisa said.

"Newsdon, can I talk to you for a second?" Rosette asked.

"Sure," I said.

We walked to the back room, and she shut the door.

"How's REBT therapy going?" she asked.

"Oh, that Albert Ellis shit?" I asked.

"It's not shit Graham," she replied.

"I know it's not shit. I'm sorry. I am doing well with it," I said.

"I can see that. I was worried when we got pulled into all of this that you were going to have a mental break again, but you seem fine. You're still not drinking?" she asked.

"You know to be honest, I used to use alcohol to numb my problems, but it turns out that alcohol was my problem. It was hard at first to stop, but to be honest, once I did, I started feeling great every day. I mean, great. I've had no need or want to have any of it in so long, I don't even think about it anymore," I replied.

"Uh huh. And what about the CBD?" she asked.

"Come on Rose. Out of all the things I could be using, CBD joints are the least of your worries. They just help take the edge off when I feel like I COULD be spiraling, which is almost never," I replied.

"I'm just worried about you. You've always been like a big brother to me, I just don't want to see anything happen. How's the medicine going?" she asked.

"Still taking it every day. Still no voices, still feeling amazing," I said.

"You know, that kind of medicine that you're on, you definitely shouldn't be drinking alcohol on it," she said.

"I know and I haven't been," I replied. "Also, I love you too girl."

We hugged for a minute until Larisa shouted out.

"Guys, get back here, I've got something," she yelped.

We came out of the bedroom.

Jackson turned to Hannah "Now it's our turn to go in the bedroom swingaling," he said.

Hannah laughed, Rosette rolled her eyes.

"OK guys, so I'll spare you the technical bullshit, but we've got a couple files here," Larisa said as she hooked the computer up to a projector on the wall. She opened the first file and in it was pictures and notes from Nikola Tesla.

"What is this?" Jean asked.

"This is the work of Nikola Tesla. Oh my God!" Jackson shrieked.

"What is it, what do you see?" I asked.

"In the late 1800's there was an Earthquake in New York City that came out of nowhere. Tesla had been living there and working on a hypothetical machine that could coalesce energy and create them. The Tesla's electro-mechanic oscillator. In 1935 at his birthday, Tesla talked about a version of his machine that caused an earthquake in downtown New York City. The media discredited it saying that it didn't do that, but his files were stolen by the CIA shortly after his death. He destroyed the machines as he did the death ray and other things not good for humanity, but it looks like the blueprints for how to make them are still here. His office in New York was raided the day after his death, and all his work was taken. It looks like someone has faithfully recreated this machine and used it to cause the Earthquakes in San Francisco and in all those other states. The thing about those other states was that they all fall on a fault line. My guess would be that they have another one of these machines and have some kind of end game planned with it," Jackson said

We looked through the files, and sure enough, there were blueprints for them. This had to be what was going on in the United States. So what. We upheave gold and they destroy the planet? This was not what I intended when I did that video with Rex.

"What are we going to do now Mansa Musa?" Rosette said to me.

"What is Mansa Musa?" Jean asked.

"It's not a what, it's a who. Mansa Musa was an African king who was the world's richest man of all time. He puts Bitchzos and Musky to shame. He had so much gold that when he had a caravan of thousands of people carrying it to make his way on the pilgrimage to Mecca I believe it was, he started just giving the gold away. What that ended up doing was devaluing the currency of the places that he visited. Which is basically what we did here," Rosette said.

"It's exactly what we did here, only back then they didn't have weapons of mass destruction, or vibration like we do today," I said.

"Uh guys, you're going to want to see this," Larisa said.

"What?" I asked.

She pointed to the projection on the wall. She had clicked on a link and then a giant clock saying 36 hours started counting down.

"Did you just activate the final countdown?" Dannick asked.

"Hold on a sec," she said as she started fumbling with the computer. "Shit,"

"What?" I asked.

"This flash drive is titled 1 of 3. Apparently these flash drives are failsafes for the plans of whoever is doing this, Hawk or whatever. Doreulla Laumilgan or Kernal or whatever must have stolen one, but not known what was on it. If this countdown was just started because one of the three of us just opened the file, then that means there is a Tesla Earthquake machine out there that is set to start cataclysmic disaster in the next 36 hours. It also means we need to get the hell out of here because I don't know if the countdown initiated a trace on us," Larisa finished.

"OK, well we know where we have to go, don't we?" Jean asked.

"We know where, but we don't know which Church. I looked it up, there are 49 churches in the area," Rosette said.

"Those Spanish, they love their Churches, don't they?" Jackson said.

"Nevermind that now, we'll figure it out on the plane. Jean, we don't have much time, how long until the plane is ready?" I asked.

"I'll make the call now, let's start heading over," Jean said as he tossed Jackson the key to the vehicle that he bought all those years back to transport us around.

"I'll go warm it up," Jackson said as he put his coat on and went downstairs.

"Alright I've put the countdown on my AquaWatch. We've got to destroy this flash drive," Larisa said.

"Give it to me," Hannah replied.

"What are you going to do with it?" Larisa said.

"Nothing, there's another file on it, don't you see?" Hannah replied.

"I didn't notice the hidden file. Good job girl," Larisa said and blew Hannah a kiss.

Rosette made a jealous face at Hannah.

"Don't worry girl, I've got plenty left in the tank for you," Larisa said and blew a kiss to Rosette.

Rosette giggled.

"So what's on this file?" Hannah asked.

"Hold on, it's encrypted too. Oh good, it's the same key as before," Larisa said.

She opened the files up on screen and it projected to the wall.

"Oh my God!" I said.

"What is it? What do you see?" Dannick asked.

"Look at these 3 files. Denver, Cairo, Antarctica, what do you know about them?" I asked everyone.

Everyone was silent.

"You all need to listen to your Blur a little more closely. These are giant and I mean giant underground cities. It looks like these people are planning on moving underground and letting the rest of the world burn to ash," I said.

"Oh my God," Rosette said.

"This is their end game, we've got 36, no, 35 hours and 15 minutes to figure this out. We've got to leave NOW!" I said.

"Great, so are we all ready to go?" Larisa asked.

"Basically, we don't have a lot of time," Rosette said.

"Hey Jean, how long is the flight to Trasmoz?" I asked.

"The pilot said 7-8 hours between the weather and everything," Jean replied.

"Crap, that leaves us basically a little more than a day to figure this all out," I replied.

We loaded our bags into the van, and Jackson took off into the night. Little did we know, we had activated the countdown and the people in charge of it we're extremely pissed off.

Any man who afflicts the human race with ideas must be prepared to see them misunderstood

—H.L. Mencken

Chapter Eighteen

34 hours until destruction

Hawk looked around at the room of his compadres. Everyone was packed and ready to go when suddenly a man came up to him.

"Sir, the countdown has been activated," the man said.

"What?! I don't remember giving authorization to do that!" He shouted.

"Sir I'm sorry, I just checked and it's down to 34 hours," the man replied.

"All right gentlemen, everybody can I have your attention please," Hawk began, "We are starting this a little earlier than we thought. You all have your boarding passes, and the planes are at the airport waiting to take you to your destinations. You all have the encrypted online file to group use, to put notes and to communicate. Our new homes are set up and we will be just fine, now please, get into the limousines outside and make your way out of here," Hawk said.

After about an hour, everybody was out of the building. There were too many secret files and computers for him to bring with them, so very methodically he started pouring gasoline on everything. After about an hour of dousing the place, he made his way to the front door. He took out his engraved zippo lighter that his father had gotten him when he turned 16 and dropped it on the patch in the front. The fire started dancing its way down the hall and up the stairs. He got in the limo. As it was pulling out, he turned back, and a giant explosion took place within the building. This startled the driver and he swerved.

"God damn it. You act like you've never heard an explosion before!" Hawk shouted.

The driver profusely apologized and kept on his way. Hawk opened up the encrypted Aqua file that people started writing in. Some were sad to leave their lap of luxury behind, actually that's what most of the posts were about. Some were talking about the location of their new home, these DUMBS as they were called by the military, deep underground military bases something or other, Hawk could not remember. He shut his laptop and relaxed for the 45-minute drive to the airport. Once there, he boarded a private Jet to Denver. He had always liked traveling alone, so he would meet up with everybody. Little did he know that one of his people had betrayed him and went to see Graham Newsdon. It was the ultimate betrayal that would have cost him his life, but even if Hawk knew about it, which he didn't, he wouldn't have time to get to him. He had to get underground quickly, otherwise he would suffer an extremely painful death.

If you want to find your tribe; speak your truth una-pologetically and see who sticks around —Unknown

Chapter Nineteen

25 hours until destruction

We had all taken a much-needed power nap on the plane. The nap turned into a few hours, and we were approaching Spain in the next 40 minutes or so.

"Hey guys, just want to let you know that we are landing at the airport in Zaragoza. There's no airport in Trasmoz," Jean said.

"Shit, well how far is it from Trasmoz?" I asked.

"About an hour, hour and 10-minute drive," Jean replied.

"Damn it! Even less time. We never should have fallen asleep. Rosette, can you find out if any of the 49 churches have a statue of Mary in them? We need to start there," I asked.

"On it," Rosette said.

"Ya, me too," Larisa replied.

We gave them a few minutes to look things up. Jackson and I were talking about the best way to spread out over Trasmoz to cover the most ground if we were going to have to search multiple churches.

"Guys, this isn't helping. There are many churches that have a statue of Mary in them, or outside of them," Rosette said.

"Damn it. Can you check the flash drive Larisa, does it show anything else?" I asked.

"Checking," she replied.

"Are things always this hectic for you?" Dannick asked me.

"Clearly, you haven't seen the movies or read the books, have you?" I questioned.

Dannick laughed.

"Hey guys, I have something!" Larisa replied.

"Thank God. What is it?" Hannah asked.

"The flash drive. The teeth. I was messing around with it and the veneer came off one of the two front teeth and exposed a tiny microchip. Hold on, let me get my equipment to see if there's anything on this," Larisa said.

We sat there incredibly impatient for a few moments while she shuffled through her suitcase until she found a plug. She placed the microchip in the converter and connected it through her flash drive. She opened it.

"No passwords, thank the Lord," she said as she smiled. Her smile quickly turned into a look of horror on her face. "You're going to want to hear this, Graham."

"What is it Larisa?" I asked.

"Remember those underground cities you were talking about?" she asked.

"Yeah, what about them?" I questioned back.

"I have a list here of members of the Quantified World Ecumenical Energy Federation. Their positions, their net worth and then there's this," she motioned for me to look.

I slid over to her and took a look. My eyes went wide. There was a list of everyone there as well as CEO's and heads of other companies and potential places they would end up. It seems that this was always their end goal, but what we had done had just sped up the process. Our system of money was incredibly broken and irrevocably unfixable, but still the thought that everyone on the planet might die except these assholes in their underground bunker really didn't sit well with me at all. Just then Jackson interrupted us.

"Uh Graham, you're going to want to see this too," he said.

"Christ, what is it?" I asked.

Jackson turned the computer around and it was Blur. In the background was a building, well, a set of buildings that were on fire. The crawl on the screen said that it was the Quantified World Ecumenical Energy

Federation. Blur was going off about how everything is all connected. Oh, if only he knew the truth.

"Guys, we have to figure this Church thing out. OK, is there a group of churches nearby where we can hustle through them?" I asked.

"No Graham, it doesn't seem like that's the deal," Larisa said.

"Anything Rose?" I asked.

"Unfortunately, nothing," she replied.

"Damn it! OK, read me the Churches names. Maybe we'll have something," I said.

"OK," Rosette said.

One by one she went through the Churches. She had been through about 30 of them when it caught my attention.

"Rosette, stop," I said.

"What?" she asked.

"Read that last one again," I replied.

"Santa Maria de la Huerta," she replied.

"That's it, that's the one we're going to," I said.

"Why?" Jean asked.

"In the excommunicated land stands Santa Maria," I replied, "haven't you guys been listening to what that man left us?" I asked.

Rosette looked at her computer quizzically. "I don't understand," she replied.

"You counted all the churches, you never actually looked at their names doll," I replied.

"I'm sorry Graham," she said.

"No time for that now. We know where we're going. We just don't know what we're looking for yet," I replied.

"Guys we're coming up on our descent into Spain," Jean replied.

"When we get there?" I asked him.

"I have a car waiting for us. I booked it as soon as I found out it was an hour away," Jean replied.

"I could just kiss you, come over here you big French man," Jackson said as he made his way towards Jean.

"Sacre bleu, I only like women you meat popsicle," Jean replied.

Rosette and Larisa both laughed.

We talked for another 20 minutes until we made our descent. We were going to have to be off to the races in order to get to where we needed to be. Little did I know just how valuable Dannick would be for us.

Innovators and creative geniuses cannot be reared in schools. They are precisely the men who defy what the school has taught them —Ludwig von Mises

Chapter Twenty

23 hours until destruction

We pulled up to Santa Maria de la Huerta and got out of the car. We cased the entire building. There was nobody waiting there with guns to protect a 'secret,' nothing. In fact, the place looked all but abandoned. When we finally got around to the side, we came across what we were looking for.

"The Zodiac stands tall. Look, there's the wheel in the sky. This has to be where we enter," I advised.

"This is definitely where we go in," Jackson replied.

We walked to the front and went in. This place is enormous.

"Alright guys, listen. The only way we're going to find the Sun beneath the Sun is if we split up like scooby doo. So I'll take Hannah and Dannick, you four go on your own," I said.

"Great idea; let's meet back here in 45 minutes," Rosette said.

"Sounds good," Hannah replied.

We split up and took opposite sides of the Church. I was surprised that for being midday, there weren't many people here at all. I guess that's what happens when the Church excommunicates your entire city. People start to give up on it. After about an hour of looking, we were exhausted. We combed our section of the Church top to bottom and there was nothing, so we decided to meet back by the giant wheel in the sky.

"I don't get it, there was supposed to be something here," I frustratingly said.

"Guys, we're under a day now that this Tesla device is going to go off. We've got to figure something out," Jackson said.

"Alright, let's swap sides. Now you guys comb our side, and we'll do yours. Maybe one of us will see something that the others missed," Dannick said.

"That's not a bad idea, OK, we'll meet back here in 45 minutes," Hannah said.

"Is it actually going to be 45 minutes, or like a Rosette 45 minutes? Jean asked.

"Shut up Solex," Rosette said.

Jean laughed to himself.

We broke up into the same groups again only this time we were on their side. Inch by inch, brick by brick we combed the entire thing until there was nothing left. As we were walking back defeated, I noticed a corridor that wasn't very prominent, they must have missed it like we almost did. Light was shining through. I walked in to find exactly what we were looking for.

"Look Hannah, Jesus the Sun, underneath it is the Sun coming through the window. The Sun beneath the Sun and it's pointing to an old-world gold. This, whatever this thing is, has to be it," I said.

I lifted the golden artifact and taped to the bottom of it was a small scroll. I took it and an alarm went off.

"Shit, we've got to get out of here," I said, as I put the scroll in my pocket and took off running.

"Hey you, stop right there!" A priest said as he took out his phone and made a call while running towards us. I called out to the others, and they came to the middle of the Church.

"Run guys!" I shouted.

Jean flicked Jackson the keys and he took off like a bolt of lightning to the car. We all trailed a few paces behind him. God this kid was fast. He got to the car and started it. We all hopped in, and he sped off, the Priest and a few parishioners with him shouting and flailing their hands. I honestly don't know if it was me removing the scroll or lifting the golden box that set the alarm off, but it didn't matter. Jackson was flooring it, and we were on our way back to the airport.

We were driving for a few miles, and everything was fine, adrenaline was subsiding until we felt someone ram the back of the car.

"Shit, they found us," Rosette hollered.

"Jax get us out of here!" I shouted.

"I'm trying guys hold on," Jackson said as he swerved into the next lane and sped up. The car behind us did the same maneuver and were speeding up to ram into us again. We were in a van, and they were in a V8. We were not getting away from them. This chase ensued for another 20 minutes.

"Guys, we have to lose them before we get to the airport or the police get notified!" Larisa shouted.

We saw a sign for a train that was about a mile up.

"Hold on guys, I have an idea," Larisa said as she took out her laptop and started furiously pounding away. "Get us to the train tracks," she commanded.

"Right away doll," Jackson said.

We were about half a mile out when the car behind us rammed into us again, this time giving us all whiplash. I turned my head which was in pain now behind us to look at the car. One of the men pulled out a shotgun and was aiming it at the back of our window.

"Guys, duck!" I shouted as everyone ducked down. The man pulled the trigger and blew the back window out of our car.

"The tracks are just ahead, what are you doing?" Jean asked Larisa.

"Jackson, floor it!" She shouted.

Jackson slammed on the gas as the gate for the train tracks started flashing colors and coming down. Jackson gritted his teeth and shot us through the gap and past the train tracks just as the gate came down. The people behind us got stuck behind it and started shaking their fists out of the window. Jackson kept his foot on the gas, and we were away from there.

"What did you do?" I asked Larisa.

"I hacked into this system and brought the gates down," Larisa said.

Don't ever let someone tell you that my friends aren't resourceful.

"Alright now, where are we going?" Jackson asked.

"Drop everybody off at the airport. I'm going to torch this car," I said.

"Are you sure Graham? Doesn't that seem a little dangerous?" Hannah asked.

"They'll be looking for it and they'll trace the car back to Jean's family if they're smart. Go to the airport, I'll meet you back at the plane in an hour," I said.

After another half an hour, we were finally at the airport. Everybody got out, and Jackson tossed me the keys.

"Are you sure you don't want me to come with you brother?" he asked.

"Actually, I could use help getting the plates and the VIN scratched off," I replied.

"Alright, so I'll come with you. Hannah, Graham. Give her the thing you recovered," Jackson said.

I handed Hannah the scroll. "Don't open it until I get back," I said, "We don't know what we're dealing with here."

"Love you," she smiled and winked at me.

Jackson and I took the car about 10 minutes away down an abandoned street. We waited until the homeless person turned the corner, and he scratched off the VIN number while I took the plates off. Finally, he tore a sleeve off his shirt, wrapped it into a wick, opened the gas cap and shoved the sleeve down. He lit his sleeve on fire and we took off running down the street and turned the corner. After a few moments we heard a loud explosion that rocked the block. Jackson and I looked at each other and started walking back the way we came from. After about an hour or so, we were back at the airport and boarded the plane.

"Great, now we're here, where's the pilot?" I asked.

"I didn't call him yet, Jean replied.

"Why not Jean? We have," I looked at my watch, "20 hours before this device goes off," I said.

"I know, but Graham, where exactly are we going?" he asked.

"Damn it! You're right. Hannah, hand me the scroll," I said.

Hannah handed it over.

I took a quick look and finally pulled the string that was keeping it rolled and it rolled out.

"What in the sweet buttery Jesus is this?" I asked.

"I have no idea," Jackson replied.

"Any ideas ladies?" I asked.

They shook their heads no.

We were running out of time, and we had this complicated map to figure out. I wasn't so sure we were going to be able to do it this time.

He who dares not offend cannot be honest

—Thomas Paine

Chapter Twenty-One

18 hours until destruction

"Come on guys we need some ideas here," I said.

"Wait, let me take a look at that," Dannick said. He was napping when we got back on the plane, and we didn't want to wake him up.

"Uh Graham, some of these are alchemical symbols," Dannick said.

"What do you mean?" I asked.

"Well, the first one is the alchemical symbol for lead. Then there is an arrow that points to the symbol for gold. So the first part is lead to gold. Then the next symbol, the downward facing triangle is the symbol for Earth, then fire. I have no idea about the rest," Dannick said as he slumped back down in his chair.

"Well, at least that's something to start with," I said.

"So, lead to gold. So they know that we were able to literally turn the 'lead' into 'gold'. So what though? That's been on the news for some time now. What about the rest?" Jackson asked.

"I don't know, but every other symbol is an arrow sign, this looks like it could be a train of thought or a map of some sorts," Rosette interjected.

"Yeah, I was thinking the same thing girl, Larisa said.

"Larisa, see if you can find any patterns on the numbers," I advised.

"On it!" Larisa said as she opened her computer and started furiously typing.

"What if they're letters?" Jean asked.

"What if they are?" I asked.

"Maybe it's an anagram," Jean replied.

I nodded my head and pulled out a pad and a pen.

HNMZTKSL -> NH

"No vowels, no this isn't it," I replied.

"Well, what about the letters at the end?" Dannick asked.

"DCC? DC Comics? Dicyclohexylcarbodiimide? Dynamic currency conversion? Direct cable connection? Digital compact cassette?" Rosette asked as she was just going down the line from the internet.

"Wait, what about dynamic currency conversion? Isn't that kind of like what we've done here?" Hannah asked.

"Could be, so then it ends up at the dynamic currency conversion. So, it starts lead to gold and ends in dynamic currency conversion?" Rosette asked.

"Wait, there's a line above the DCC," I said.

Everybody looked dejected as it looked like we were starting from scratch.

"Rosette, while Larisa runs numbers, can you please search if there's something with DCC with a line above it? Maybe it's a symbol or a passcode to something. Larisa, I need you to look into gematria, the Hebrew alphabet as well. Anything that could be scrambled with these numbers," I said.

"On it Newsdon," Rosette said.

"Absolutely," Larisa replied.

They snuggled up next to each other and started typing away at the computer. After a few minutes Rosette scared the shit out of us.

"I think I got something on the DCC Graham!" She yelped.

"What, what is it?" I asked.

"It's Roman numerals," she replied.

"What do you mean?" I asked.

"DCC is 700, but when you put a line over the top, it becomes 700,000," she replied.

"So that's 700,000?" I asked.

"That's what I'm trying to tell you Graham!" She yelled back.

"Alright relax, listen I'm just as nervous and frustrated as the rest of you are. OK so once again, Dannick, take us through this," I said.

Dannick stood up and cleared his throat. "Lead into gold into a set of numbers into a smaller set of numbers into Earth into fire into 700,000. Wait guys, what if the Earth arrow fire means that Earth will be consumed with fire?" he asked.

I looked at him.

"That's a real possibility, but what's up with the 700,000?" I asked.

"Could it be like the 144,000 in Revelation that you talk about Graham?" Hannah asked.

"The 144,000 are not actually the amount of people that get to go to Heaven, they have to do with the chakras, but I don't know," I said.

"Could it have to do with the Georgia Guidestones that want to keep people under 500,000,000?" Jean asked.

"How do you get five hundred million to seven hundred thousand?" I asked.

"Je ne sais pas, I'm trying to help here," Jean said.

"Larisa, we need all combinations of ideas for this. Check for the 14 and the 8 first. Maybe if we figure out the smaller part, we can crack the larger numbers," I said.

"The first set of numbers add up to 123," Rosette quipped.

"Sacred numerology?" I asked as I turned away from everyone. I had this ball of fire in my stomach with this constant worry that what we had done could have caused the end of the world and it would have been our fault. We had to figure this out.

"Any ideas?" Jackson asked me.

"Jax, do these numbers or any of these numbers mean anything in physics to you? Do you see any patters within this?" I asked.

"At last, the day has come where you ask for my physics advice," Jackson said.

"Jax please, I'm so nervous right now I'm about to take an adrenaline shit that's going to ground the plane for a month," I replied.

"Right, give me your pad and pen, I'll try and figure this out," Jackson said.

"Rosette, can you find anything with the number 700,000? Is it money? People? Historical number? Look back 700,000 years, see if you can find any patterns," I said as I went into the back of the plane to the bathroom to take my stress shit.

I sat down on the toilet and closed my eyes. I can't remember the last time I was by myself with a moment to myself. Not since my kid was born, not since we all got back together for this insanity. I was only in for 2 minutes before I heard a knock on my door.

"Graham, get the fuck out here," Jackson said.

Of course I can't even shit in peace.

"Coming!" I yelled back.

"I have something bud, you're a genius," Jackson said.

I washed my hands and came out of the bathroom. I looked at Jackson.

"The numbers aren't random at all, they're chemicals," he said.

"What? I don't understand." I replied.

"The periodic table of elements. I couldn't find anything in physics, so I thought chemistry maybe. This has to be it. Listen. 8 14 13 26 20 11 19 12. On the periodic table those are oxygen, silicon, aluminum, iron, calcium, sodium, potassium, magnesium. Rosette, look up what those put together create," Jackson said.

"One sec. Ok, ok, ok, ok, oh my God!" Rosette shrieked.

"What is it?" I asked.

"These are the chemicals that make up a volcano," Rosette said.

"A volcano? Are you sure?" I asked.

"Yes, and the other two numbers are silicon and oxygen. Together they make up lava. The device must be at a volcano. They're planning on causing an earthquake at a volcano, triggering it to spew lava everywhere. The map we have. Turning lead to gold lead them to a volcano and the lava which will turn the earth into fire. Now we just need to know what the last part is," Rosette said.

"Did you find anything about the 700,000? This has to be a clue as to where to go. We're so close and we can't even get this plane off the ground to go where we need to. Come on guys THINK!" I shouted.

Dannick looked at us and walked over to Rosette, he pointed to her computer, and she gave it to him, he bowed and thanked her then went back to his seat. He was very quiet and very engaged with the computer, none of us could say a word, until finally he cracked the code 10 minutes later.

"Guys, every 700,000 years Yellowstone explodes. We have tracked it back to evidence 2.1 million years ago, then again 1.4 million years ago then finally last one was 700,000 years ago. A lot of conspiracy theories online think that it's overdue. If this were to explode it would at the very least cover the entire United States with ash from the wind, at the worst it could destroy the planet. If Tesla's device is allowed to go off there, it will jigger the volcano to epic proportions and destroy us all, while those bastards live in the underground," Dannick said.

"Jean, call the pilot, we've got to head to Wyoming. Shit, how much time do we have?" I asked.

"A little over 16 hours," Hannah said.

"Damn it, that'll give us anywhere from 4-6 hours to find it. I have to email the President," I said.

"You still have his email address?" Jean asked.

"Of course I do," I replied.

After about half an hour the pilot showed up and Jean brought him into the cockpit and spoke to him for a few moments. When he came out, he told us to fasten our seatbelts. Within another 15 minutes we were up in the air. I opened the computer to start my email to Rand Dotplum who was in his second term as president after we figured out the poison vaccine and he presided over the cleanup; he ran away with his reelection.

Dear Rand,

It's me Graham. I know you haven't heard from me in quite some time, but we need your help. After we were able to show that you could actually literally turn lead into gold, or more specifically a meteorite,

the markets and the financials went to hell. There's too much for me to explain right now and I promise I will fill you in when I get the chance. Just know that the Quantified World Ecumenical Energy Federation is behind the Earthquakes in the United States. I even know where they all are, but for now it's important that you send the military and the national guard to Yellowstone. They had stolen Tesla blueprints for an earthquake machine that he came up with once he died. Someone within the FBI had provided them to Hawk Cublass and his people. You saw what it did on the fault line in the Midwest and what it did in San Francisco. If this goes off at Yellowstone, we are all as good as dead. It will basically block out the sun. You can reach me at this email address, but we are on our way there right now to help look for this. Please go on a limb and trust me, I've never steered you wrong before.

Yours truly,
Graham Newsdon

I hit the send button and closed the computer. My stomachache was starting to go away a bit, not much, but I tried to get a few hours of sleep during our flight. Yeah right, no chance at that. I sat there with my eyes closed while everybody talked about their ideas of where this device was located. That was the final piece of the puzzle. Where is this thing, and when we find it, what are we going to do with it.

I didn't say it would be easy, I just said it would be the truth —Morpheus from the Matrix

Chapter Twenty-Two

6 hours until destruction

My computer sent me an alert saying I received a new message.

Graham,

It is great to hear from you, I've been following your career. You've been very busy so I can see. You know that up until 1913, Americans kept all of their earnings. Despite this, we still had schools, colleges, roads, vast railroads, streets, subways, the Army, Navy and the Marine Corps. Since its inception, the Federal Reserve has presided over the loss of 99% of the value of the dollar and dealing with them was going to be the last thing on my agenda. I had to be very careful, because the last two Presidents that tried to print money ended up losing their lives. Even Andrew Jackson who tried it had two assassination attempts on his life. We

need to reform this, and I had a plan to tax the Fed at .0006% until we put them out of business. However, this is a conversation for another time. What you have emailed me is incredibly disturbing, but I'm not surprised. After your video came out with the gold, we ran ideas and knew this kind of thing was a possibility. I saw the second email you sent me in the middle of the night about the underground locations. I have co-ordinated with other Presidents and Prime Ministers across the country, and we have decided that we are going to let them live there. I have dispatched teams to Antarctica, Denver, Egypt, and every place you have mentioned to find these locations and to seal them in. They are under the impression that the world is ash and smoke, and we will let them think as such. This we are keeping a secret from the people, so they never really know what happened otherwise it will cause worldwide chaos. We're literally going to bury them alive and move on with society.

What you have said to me about Yellowstone is incredibly disturbing. I know by now not to question you when you come to me with something important and I have dispatched 2000 troops with metal detectors to Yellowstone to scan as much of the area as they can in hopes of finding Tesla's machine. Our government should have never raided his offices, if they hadn't, this device's blueprint would never have been stolen and given to those at the Federation. What comes around, goes around it seems doesn't it, Graham?

I know you are on your way to Yellowstone right now, but I must implore you not to come. I know you probably won't listen, but if we don't get to this in time, there could be catastrophic consequences and the chances are that you all may die. I implore you to go back home to Boston and live your lives like nothing is happening. I've discussed this with my cabinet and the joint chiefs, and we have decided to not leak this to the media as it would cause countrywide chaos, and for what? If this erupts, we are all dead anyway, best not to scare the shit out of people before hand. Please keep this to yourselves as well.

If you end up coming to Yellowstone, the person in charge is a man named Kaolin Slate. Ask for him and he will bring you up to speed.

I can't stop you from coming, but I can say that your help in discovering this plot has been indispensable to your country and to the world. It's a shame you can never get credit for it. After this is all said and done, we are going to redefine currency and what has value. The banks have been pressuring our country since its inception by the you know who's. I had planned on doing this in 18 months towards the end of my second term, but you have just sped up the timeline. I wish you all the best Graham, give your wife and your friends my love.

Yours faithfully,
President Rand Dotplum

I sat for a minute and let this letter sink in. I passed my laptop around so that everybody else could read this. I couldn't believe the chain of events that completing an impossible alchemical procedure had triggered on the world. One by one they all read the letter. By the time

Dannick, who was last, finished it, they turned back to me.

"So this might be it guys," Dannick said.

"What do you mean?" Rosette asked.

"In six hours or less, we could end up being covered in ash and lava and end up like the bodies in Pompeii," Dannick finished.

I had been shot, I had been tortured, I had been abused, I had a mental breakdown. I had survived all of this, but there was a lagging feeling in my head that I wouldn't survive this one. I felt something in my pocket as I started fidgeting around. It was the ball of gold from the lab. I took it out and started playing with it. It was unlike any kind of gold I had ever seen, it put my diamond encrusted chain link wedding band to shame. I put it back in my pocket and turned to everyone.

"Jean, how much time left?" I asked.

"The clock says five hours and forty minutes," he replied.

"For the flight Jean," I replied.

"Oh right; hold on, I'll check," he said as he made his way to the cockpit.

"Baby, I just wanted to say that if things go sideways here, I will find you in the afterlife," Hannah said.

"Don't think like that. But yes, our energies never die, and I will find your energy again," I replied.

"Now you're starting to talk physics finally," Jackson said.

"We're touching down in 15 minutes," Jean replied.

"Great," I said.

I started my routine. I put a piece of gum in my mouth and earplugs in my ears. I closed my eyes and focused deeply on what we were about to do. We had to hit the ground running. Even if we did find this device, how were we going to get it far away enough in time? How could we destroy it? Questions started flooding my mind until I felt my ears pop as we descended. I hate this part of flying. I started forcing myself to yawn and chewed the gum. My ears popped back. After about 20 minutes of this, we had touched down. Jean as always had a vehicle waiting for us. This was going to be the final stand of all stands and we were going to need all the help we could get.

There comes a time when one must take a position that is neither safe, nor politic, nor popular, but he must take it because conscience tells him it is right—Dr. King

Chapter Twenty-Three

Northwest Wyoming 4 hours 20 minutes until destruction

We sped to Yellowstone. It took us some time to get there, there weren't many places to land in Wyoming. When we got there, we met up with some of the military. Once I told one of them my name, they ran off to get Kaolin. After about fifteen minutes he came running towards us.

"Graham, it's a pleasure to meet you, although I wish it was under different circumstances. You know I was there when Lilac gave you the medal for your brother all those years ago," Kaolin said.

"I didn't know that. Thank you for being there," I said.

"Your brother was a true hero. I met him only once. We were on a mission together very early on before he got recruited to the secret mission. We played Texas Hold Em. He beat the shit out of me. He figured out my tells instantly; he had a real eye for that," Kaolin said.

"I can't remember growing up ever beating him in poker, or uno, or any type of card game. He was truly great," I said.

"I'll never know why he never entered any poker tournaments and joined the Marines instead," Kaolin replied.

"Our parents were very strict in their religion. They believed gambling was a sin and would never have let him do that," I replied.

"Well, rest his soul. I have brought you some metal detectors," Kaolin said as he handed a few out to my friends, "we are in the upper quadrant, there's some a few clicks away from the supervolcano itself. If you wanted to check the down and left areas, that would be helpful. We have cars and choppers parked at the entrance to the park," he said.

"I know, we saw them when we parked. Is this your getaway plan?" I asked.

"Getaway from what? We're all screwed if this machine goes off and the volcano erupts. Let's just pray that we find something," he said as he saluted us and ran off.

"Alright guys, where do you want to start?" I asked.

"Should we split up?" Dannick asked.

"This might be the last time we ever see each other. Let's stay together. Let's go south," I said.

We walked for about twenty minutes until we saw an area of disturbed ground.

"Let's start here," Rosette said.

"Makes sense," Hannah replied.

"Larisa, is there anything that you can run on your computer that can access an overhead of the park where we can see if any ground has been disturbed?" I asked.

"On it," Larisa said as she sat down on the ground and crossed her legs and went to work.

We started hovering the metal detectors over the land. A few times it went off and we dug, only to find some coins, or other scraps of metal. This wasn't looking very promising. After half an hour of this I stopped.

"Guys, there's nothing here," I said.

"Should we go to the other area of the park they said they needed help?" Jean asked.

"We've covered this entire area already. Larisa, do you have anything?" I asked.

"I see some freshly disturbed ground in the area of the park over to the left," she said.

"Did you hack into the satellite system?" Hannah asked.

"I deny all accusations completely," she said.

"Great, well let's go," I said.

We walked for another 40 minutes. Don't let anyone tell you that Yellowstone is a small park; this shit is absolutely enormous.

2 hours and 50 minutes until destruction

"There's nothing here guys either?" I said.

"This place is just too big to comb through," Jackson said as we looked over and saw some of the military checking the grounds not far from us.

"At least we have them helping," Hannah said.

"More people just means more casualties," I replied.

"You can't think like that Graham, we still have time," Larisa said.

"Wait. What if it's not buried here, but it's hidden in a building," Jackson said.

"What building?" I asked.

"The hotel near Old Faithful," he replied.

"What is Old Faithful?" Jean asked.

"It's a geyser. We have to go now if we're going to go," Jackson said.

"Alright let's go, it's worth a shot," I said.

We made our way to the hotel, bringing one of the military men with us. We explained to him the situation along the way, and he agreed. When we got to the hotel, he explained it to the head of the hotel, and they unlocked all the doors and evacuated the people within it.

One by one we checked every room, but there was absolutely nothing. That was until we hit the very last room. The most expensive room with a view of the geyser. I was checking the room, and nothing was out of the ordinary until I found a picture under the bed that must have been left by one of the people who was staying in the room. It was a flyer of Yellowstone attractions and had the entrance sign of the park circled in black marker. A chill ran down my spine. Whoever stayed in this room did a horrible job of covering their tracks and this might just be the key to saving us all. This entrance sign was right when we came into the park. I ran out of the room and grabbed everyone.

"Guys, we have to go. I'm pretty sure it's around here," I said as I showed them the flyer.

I can get us there in no time," the military man said.

We left the hotel and hopped into his car, some got in the back of the truck. We took off. It was freezing cold out, but we got to the front in no time. As I suspected, some of the ground near the sign was disturbed.

1 hour 40 minutes until destruction

"Alright guys, we don't have a lot of time left, so get cracking. Larisa, see if you can find some time lapsed photos of people being here. We know from the hotel clerk that the room I was in was rented out two days ago, so go back about a day and a half to two days ago and see if we can find people around it," I said.

"Roger that," she said as she went to work.

We started checking the area and it went off like a Christmas tree. We dug up what we could find with the shovels from the military vehicle, and we stopped when we saw what it was.

It was a ring of C4 explosives with a timer on it for 3 hours.

"Why would they set an explosion after the volcano was set to erupt?" I asked.

"Because the device is around here and they want to destroy all evidence of it. Fuck, I have to call this in," the military man said as he radioed into Kaolin.

"We have about 20 minutes until they arrive," the man said.

"We kept searching the area for another 15 minutes, until I put the spear into the ground.

"Guys there's nothing here. Goddamnit this is so frustrating," I said as I walked up to the sign and punched it as hard as I could. Damn it, that hurt. But I noticed something. The shield flapped open then closed.

"Guys, I might have something," I said, as I lifted the plaque.

THERE IT WAS!

The device was a lot smaller than I thought it would be, but a home had been carved into the sign for it. I pulled it out.

"Is that what I think it is?" Hannah asked.

"I can't tell, it's covered by something. Jax come here!" I shouted.

"What is it brother?" he asked.

"What is this material covering it?" I asked.

He took it from my hands and looked at it.

"Hannah, I need your ring," he said.

"Why?" I asked.

"Because Diamond is the hardest thing on earth. I need to see if I can crack this thing," he said.

She handed over her ring.

He took it and used all his power to try and crack it, but to no avail.

"What's harder than diamond?" I asked.

"This has to be a graphene case," he replied.

"What's graphene?" Hannah asked as she put her ring back on and checked it to make sure it wasn't scratched.

"It has many uses. I would take an elephant balancing on a pencil on a sheet of paper thick of graphene to break it. This is airtight," he said.

"So, we can't throw it in the volcano?" Jean asked.

"It wouldn't do anything to it," Jackson said.

"So, what can we do?" Rosette asked.

"We can't dent it, we can't submerge it. It's perfectly encased. I have no idea," Jackson said.

We could hear the military in the distance making their way towards us.

"Guys, I need you all to get away from the bombs," the military man said.

We started walking towards the cars feeling defeated. To come so close, only for it to be so far. This was heart wrenching. I stuck my hands in my pocket because they were freezing. This douche forgot to bring gloves with him. When I put my hand in my pocket, I felt something that I forgot I had. It was the gold ball. I took it out and looked at it and looked at everybody else. The military stopped what they were doing and looked at me as well. I looked at it, then back at the graphene case. I figured why not. I slammed the gold ball into it as hard as I could and to my surprise, a piece of it flew off.

"Graham, this gold has properties that we've never seen before on Earth, keep hitting it," Jean said.

"Give it to me Graham," Jackson said.

I wasn't about to argue with a rhino, so I did. He swung his arm back and slammed the gold into it as hard as he could. Another piece chipped off.

"Keep going Jackson!" Dannick yelled.

Jackson kept at it for a few minutes, but you could see it was taking its toll on him. Unfortunately, only some of the surface layer came off. He gave it one last heave and landed a decent size hole in the graphene box. We stood back looking at it. We couldn't bury it; we couldn't throw it in the volcano, there wasn't time. I picked up my phone and searched something.

"Guys, I know what we have to do, but we have to leave right now. It's 20 miles away," I said.

Everybody stopped and looked at me. The military looked like they were going to make a move, so I turned and started running towards the cars and the helicopters. Everyone trailed a few steps behind me, the military about 20 seconds behind them. We were just going to make it if we left now. We all piled into the car, and I screamed at Jean.

"Drive!" I shouted.

"Where?" he asked.

"Just get us to a main road and follow this GPS. I have an idea. Jax, keep hammering at this thing," I said.

Every man is a creature of the age in which he lives, and few are able to raise themselves above the ideas of the time —Voltaire

Chapter Twenty-Four

30 minutes until destruction

We sped down the road with the military in close pursuit.

"Now would be a good time for you to tell me where we're going friend," Jean said.

"Just follow my GPS, here," I said as I handed him my phone.

"I hope you know what you're doing Graham," Hannah said.

"If I'm wrong, we won't be around much longer anyway," I replied.

Jean drove down the road as we watched the miles tick down on the MAPS app. The military were in pursuit, but that was it. They couldn't call the police because then they would have to share the reason for them being in the area, and that would start a cataclysm with the police and the news and the world news that they didn't want as much as we didn't want. So they kept behind us and followed us.

"Graham, where are we going?" Jackson asked.

"How's the box coming along?" I asked.

"I've got the top right corner exposed," Jackson said.

"Good, you can stop. We only need that," I replied.

"For what?" Jackson asked.

"Yeah, where are we going?" Rosette asked.

"We're going to Yellowstone Lake," I replied.

"What do you mean the lake? It's frozen," Dannick said.

"We're going to have to punch a hole into it and drop this device in the middle of it," I replied.

"How is that going to help anything?" Larisa asked.

"Because, we have a hole in the graphene box now. Once this is submerged, the water will destroy the machine, then it will sink to the bottom of the lake never to be seen again" I said.

Everybody looked at me like I had a giant dick growing out of my forehead.

"Jackson, please explain," I said.

"Graham is right. If we had just dropped the entire box into the water, the graphene would have protected the device, however now that we punched a hole in it, the entire container should fill with water and destroy the machine," Jackson said.

5 miles out, 15 minutes before destruction

"Come on Jean, step on it," Rosette said.

"I am Rose, believe me I am," he replied.

I looked behind us, the military has seemed to have given up running us off the road and instead were following us in a single file line. I figured they were going to arrest us once we got out of the car, then maybe I could explain to them what we were doing. I didn't have time for that, we were within 13 minutes until this device went off.

"Just so you all know, if this doesn't work and the device goes off, it's going to run a vibratory frequency that will make you shit your pants. That's the last thing you'll remember before you're covered in lava," Jackson said.

"Charming," Larisa said as she turned to the GPS. It said we were 1 minute out.

"OK guys, so here's what we're going to do. Jackson and Graham will take the device and a shovel to make a hole in the ice, we'll block the military. By the time they're done with us, this should be done," Hannah said.

I turned to Hannah. She wasn't usually one to bark orders, but I guess the threat of being extinguished in a flash turned it on for her.

7 minutes 34 seconds until destruction

Jean parked the car and we all got out. Jackson and I took off towards the lake and the others turned around and flagged the military down. I couldn't turn to see what was happening to them, but knowing them, they were put in zip tie handcuffs and put in the car.

"Graham, what are you doing brother?" One of the men shouted at me.

"I'm sorry, this is the only way!" I shouted back.

"Let's talk about this. You don't need to do this," the man said as he raised his gun up at me. I froze.

"Jackson now!" I said as I pushed him as hard as I could into the middle of the lake. He slammed the shovel down as hard as he could and broke a small hole.

"I'm sorry, I have to," I said as I turned and dropped the device into the water.

All of a sudden there was a flash of light that came from under the ice. Then the ice started to crack.

"Run Jax!" I shouted as he dropped his shovel into the water, and we took off. The ice spider cracked all the way across, and then suddenly shattered with an explosion as the ice went into the water. Then just as quickly as that happened, the water was calm. The countdown was up, and we didn't feel any vibrations. I didn't shit my pants yet, so that was a good sign.

"I'm sorry, I couldn't, I didn't have time to explain it to you guys so that you could play politics with it. Can you let my friends go now?" I asked.

Kaolin stepped out of one of the Humvees. He walked slowly up to me with his walkie talkie.

"This is Kaolin, report on the status of the volcano," he calmly stated into the walkie talkie.

"All quiet on the Western Front!" The reply came back in.

Kaolin handed his walkie talkie to the man that was pointing a gun at us earlier and walked up to us.

"This country and this planet owe you and your friends a great deal of gratitude. How did you know this would work?" he asked.

"I didn't. There have been a few variations of Tesla's Earthquake machine, I was just praying this one couldn't handle water," I replied.

Kaolin smiled at me, then turned to Jackson.

"You know big boy, there's always room for a guy like you in the United States Military," he said.

Jackson laughed.

"I'm ok brother man," Jackson said.

Kaolin shrugged his shoulders and turned back to me. "You guys were never here. Head back to your car, get on your plane and go back home. We'll figure it out while you're gone," Kaolin said as he looked dead seriously into my eyes. He then turned to his military brethren and nodded. At once, two of the vehicles opened and my friends came out. The army men cut the zip ties, and they ran over to us.

"What are you going to tell them?" I asked.

"I have no idea yet. Oh Graham, one more thing," Kaolin said as he pointed to my pocket.

I reached into it and pulled out the gold ball.

"We're going to need to confiscate that. We need to get it to our labs to study it," Kaolin said.

I slumped. Then I perked right back up. What was I going to do? Walk into a bank? An OTB? I had no use for this. I tossed it to him, and he caught it.

"Graham," Kaolin said.

"Yes?" I asked.

"Take care of yourself," he said as he smiled and tipped his hat to me.

I walked up to Hannah and gave her a kiss, then brought everyone in for a group hug.

"Let's pray this is the very last time anything ever happens to us," Rosette said.

"Amen to that," Jackson said.

"Actually, when you say Amen, you're actually giving praise to Amun-Ra," I replied.

Jackson stared at me blankly.

"Stand right there, I'm just going to get this shovel real quick," he said.

I laughed.

We all started walking back to the car. We made the 90-minute drive back to the airport and hopped on board.

"Back to Boston?" Jean asked.

"Sight for sore eyes. Yes actually, I'm still going to be able to make my lecture at the TD Bank Arena in a couple of days," I replied.

"You sold out the TD Bank Arena?" Dannick asked wide eyed.

"It's not that hard. The Celtics manage to do it on occasion too," I replied.

Dannick laughed.

I sat in my seat and closed my eyes. We were safe, at least for the near foreseeable future.

The world may never understand you. That is not your fault. That is your gift —Unknown

Chapter Twenty-Five

I opened my computer and saw an email from the President. I gathered everyone around me and read it to them.

Dear Graham and friends,

I can't thank you enough for what you've done. We are indebted to you over and over again. Henry David Thoreau said 'Rather than love, than money, than fame, give me truth. I think that's appropriate here. Kaolin brought me up to speed with what you've done. It takes a lot of guts to go against the grain, let alone the US military and do what you did. You have saved us all. Unfortunately, as I've previously mentioned, the world can never know what you and your friends have done. It's just safer that way. The world is a very big place Graham, and as far as those who participated in

this, we have located their hideaways and have sealed them in. As far as the public knows, they have stepped down, cashed out and are living their lives in private islands. We intend to keep it that way.

The Federal Reserve is a cartel, it's a banking cartel. And like all cartels, it only has one purpose and that is to serve the benefit of the members of the cartel, period. That was G. Edward Griffin. In a few days I'm going to make an announcement that we are going to start taxing the Federal Reserve until we have paid our debt off and then put them out of business. I expect that many people will come after me for this. Unlike when Lincoln and Kennedy tried to print their own money and were killed for it, they didn't have social media and eyes on them from around the world. I intend to do some interviews where I explain our decision. This is long overdue, and your help has been invaluable. In light of this new gold that you have created, we're going to start after the Fed is put out of business to move towards crypto. It's time for this and it's time we stop pretending not to. We are in the Age of

Aquarius, which according to you is when man evolves, and that's what I intend to do with the rest of my Presidency.

I will always have the same email in case you need to reach out to me or just want to check in. I'm saddened by the fact that we cannot have a public ceremony for you and your friends for what you've done, but we cannot afford the publicity of the fact that the world was almost ended due to the Quantified World Ecumenical Energy Federation. We have dealt with those that were in charge of that creation.

If you ever need anything, please feel free to ask. And good luck on your final lecture at the TD Bank Arena. I wish I could be there.

Sincerely yours,
Rand Dotplum, President

I finished reading it to everyone and they were all silent until Jean spoke up.

"I can't believe it," he said.

"What?" I asked.

"The Quantified World Ecumenical Energy Federation. The QWEEF. We beat the QWEEF!" he said.

We all stared at him.

"Can, can you say that one more time?" I asked holding back a fit of laughter.

"What did I say? I said we took down the QWEEF!" He shouted.

Rosette and Larisa giggled.

"I don't understand. What is so bad about saying we destroyed the QWEEF?" he asked.

We all couldn't hold it anymore. We erupted in a fit of laughter.

"Jean baby, do you know what that is?" Larisa asked.

"I do not know what you're talking about," Jean said.

Larisa sauntered her way over to Jean and whispered in his ear. Jeans face turned to horror.

"Mon dieu, what have I said?" Jean asked.

Again, we erupted in laughter.

"Hey guys we're about to make our descent into Boston," the pilot said over the loudspeaker.

Here we go again. I popped a piece of gum in my mouth and put in ear plugs. I closed my eyes for the remaining few minutes we were in the air. I was thinking to myself how much I missed my boy. I wished that I hadn't left him with family, but he wouldn't have had a chance to grow up into a man had we not chased this lead and done what we had done, so I was focusing on that thought instead. The next few days were going to be intense as in 48 hours I was going to headline the TD Bank Arena with my lecture. I started shifting my focus towards that.

A good teacher should shatter your illusions and leave you, at least initially, very frustrated and confused
—Unknown

Final Chapter

I took a sip of water and stared out to the crowd that filled up TD Bank to hear my presentation. All 19,580 people. Packed to the gills. I took another sip of water. The air smelled of pot. Must be from last night's OAR concert.

"OK, before I begin, I want to share a thing with you. This will be the last show I do for a while. I wanted to end it in Boston, my hometown," I paused and looked out to the crowd. I can't believe I sold out a stadium for my work. "I know that people told you to turn your phones off and no pictures, but I don't care about that. Turn them back on. Film this if you want. Share this with everybody that you can. Take pictures. Before I begin, can you guys make some noise?" I asked.

The crowd went apeshit.

Wow. So this is what it feels like to be a rockstar. "Alright everyone, let's begin," I said as I put the first slide up. "Employ your time in improving yourself by other men's writings so that you shall come easily by what others have labored hard for. That's Socrates, thousands of years ago, and to be honest it's very fitting for what I'm going to share with all of you. I've been working on decoding texts and studying them for years. It got me far in life, I've made a lot of enemies along the way because of it. Now, Astrology is the oldest science on earth," I said as I switched to the next slide. "It goes back as far as I can see to the Lascaux Caves. Now the Lascaux Caves are called that because they are in Lascaux France. Makes sense, doesn't it? They are caves that teenagers went into, much like how we found the Dead Sea Scrolls, a youngling went into the cave and found the jars. In the Lascaux Caves, these teens went deep into them, and in the back of the cave they found this," I said as I switched to the next slide.

"Now as you can see, you see the bulls on the top, the many faces of the lion on the right and the horse on the bottom left. Now in Astrology, the Bull is Taurus, the Lion is Leo, and the Horse is Sagittarius, it's just missing the man with the bow and the arrow. What they did was they carbon dated the wall and it came out to 40,000 years plus or minus 5,000 years. Now the 'young Earth' crowd would have you believe that carbon dating is inaccurate and does not work, and to their credit, that's sort of 'half-true.' The truth is that up to 50,000 years, carbon dating is incredibly accurate, however past that when you get into the hundreds of thousands and millions of years it falls off a bit. So they then brought in an Astronomer with a computer, because they noticed the correlations, and he rewound the sky back 40,000 years, because we can do that with computers now. When they printed out what they saw and superimposed it onto the wall, they found that the constellations lined up perfectly with the paintings. Not only that, but they also found that on June 21st and only on June 21st, the Summer Solstice, the Sun's light came into the cave and bounced off the walls." I paused for a second to take a sip of water. My eyes were drawn to a man sitting in the front row, all in black with his hoodie up. He had a long black beard with hints of grey in it and piercing brown eyes. He seemed very out of place from the usual crowd I draw, and I don't know why I happened to notice him. Something felt off. But he was smiling and filming me, so I let it go. "Now, there are questions you can ask which confuse people and are up for much debate in the Bible. Questions such as 'How Jesus was able to heal the blind, how he walked on water, how he turned water into wine, why he had 12 disciples, why he was betrayed with a kiss by Judas, why he was dead for 3 days, why is his birthday on December 25th,' now all of that can be explained with astrology or Astrotheology, but in order to do that, I need to go over the 12 signs with you. So let's begin," I said.

"I start with the sign Aquarius, even though Aries is the start of the year. Aquarius is represented by the man with the water pitcher and this story goes back to Zeus and the Greeks. Zeus was looking down on earth and he saw a young 14-year-old boy that he thought was beautiful and that he wanted up in Heaven with him. His father did not want to let him go, so Zeus bargained with him, gave him livestock, etc, and eventually was allowed to take the boy up. Once the boy got up there, he was made to feed the Gods with Ambrosia which is the nectar of the Gods out of the water pitcher. After a while he got fed up with doing that, and one day he poured the pitcher over the side of Heaven, and by doing so he flooded the Earth. This is where the Greeks get their flood story from. Zeus was furious and was going to punish the boy, but in a moment of self-reflection he realized that he made the boy come up against his will. Instead of punishing him, he immortalized him as the man with the water pitcher pouring it out or the constellation Aquarius. So, every time you hear the words 'son of man,' 'man,' 'baptism, because this is how you baptize someone with the water jug and pouring it out onto the baby's head,' 'water pitcher,' 'fountain,' 'stream,' 'river,' 'pond,' 'lake,' they're talking about the water in

Aquarius. Now, it's important to know that the sign Aquarius in Astrology is an Air Sign. However, because there is water in the sign, it can be used to signify water. Pisces is the sign of the two fish in the water. All previous water examples apply here as well. So, the first two signs that I speak about are 'water signs.' Then Aries is the Ram. In Aries you have March 21st, which is the Spring Equinox, it's a 12-hour day, 12-hour night. In Aries you have the Passover and Easter. Now, in Judaism the Passover is when God metaphorically passes over Egypt and smites the first-born sons of anyone who doesn't have the lamb, or the Ram's blood smeared on their doorpost. However, in Astrology the Passover is literally when the Sun 'passes over' the Equinox and begins its ascent back up to its height in the summer solstice. In Christianity the passive over is changed and becomes the 'Resurrection of God's Son/Sun'. So the 'pass over' and the 'resurrection' are two ways of saying the same thing about the Sun. Everyone who's ever heard me speak knows that Jesus represents the Sun, and that each story in the Bible is a different way of speaking about the Sun and its journey, or the Zodiac signs. So whenever you hear the words ram, lamb, shepherd, ram's horn, they're talking about Aries. Next is Taurus, the Bull. When you look at the sky and see Taurus during its season, you know, as above so below. You see the Bull in the sky, you need to put the plow on the Bull on Earth and plow and plant so you can harvest later in the year. We have machinery that does the plowing now, but back in the day, these ancients relied on the bull. So whenever you hear bull, ox, calf, or cow, because a cow is a female bull, they're talking about Taurus. Next, Gemini is the twins. It's the story of Castor and Pollux Troy, who's sister was Helen of Troy. It's the story of Achilles, another Greek story. Whenever you hear twins or brothers, they're talking about Gemini. Next, Cancer is the crab and it's the sideways moving creature. So what the Sun does is starting on December 25th it rises a degree on its axis. The following day an additional degree, the following day another degree and so on and so forth until it hits June 21st which is the Summer Solstice. The Sun is at its height and doesn't rise anymore, it's the longest day of the year and the shortest night. Then after June 21st, just like the crab, it walks sideways for 3 days which it stays at that height. On June 25th it lowers a degree, then the following day another degree, then another degree until it hits December 21st which is the lowest point. It's the winter solstice, the longest night, shortest day of the year. It's when the Sun doesn't rise above the horizon, so the ancients used to say that the Sun was dead. Then, it walks sideways for 3 days like it did in the Summer, so this became 'God's Sun was dead for 3 days.' Then on December 25th, it rises again, the Sun is 'Born Again,' the 'light of the world.' 'the only begotten Son/Sun.' So, anytime you hear crab or beetle, they're talking about Cancer. Now the Beetle part is interesting because in the ancient Egyptian Zodiac, the crab was actually the scarab beetle. It's why St. Augustine called Jesus 'The Good Beetle." The other change in the Zodiac from the Egyptians was that the Sphinx took place of the Lion. But aside from those two changes, the Zodiac has pretty much stayed the same. Next is Leo, the lion. The lion is the king of the jungle. The ruling planet of Leo is actually the Sun. Whenever you hear lion, lioness, cub, they're talking about Leo. Then Virgo is the virgin/lady holding the wheat stalk. So remember before when I said that you plant in Taurus, well the virgins would go out into the field and cultivate the wheat in Virgo in order to make the bread. So whenever you hear virgin, wheat, grain, seed, barley, corn, grainy things that you harvest in Virgo, they're talking about Virgo. Now, Libra is the justices. It's the scales, the balance. The reason it's the justice or the judgment is because it 'judges' God's Sun as it passes over the fall Equinox and is sentenced to begin its descent into winter, into cold, into death. Because Libra is the judgment, it's clear to see why the Jewish people, 8 days after Rosh Hashanah, celebrate Yom Kippur, which is in Libra. It's the day of 'judgment' where they fast from food and drink and pray all day that God will keep them in the book of life for another year. So whenever you hear law, judge, justice, divorce, marriage, court, or 'law things,' they're talking about Libra. Libra is also Wine season.' I paused for a moment and took another sip of water. "All the ladies here that like to go to vineyards," I said as half the crowd started screaming, "You go in the springtime but that's stupid. In the spring the vines are bare and empty. If you go in Libra during September/October, you will see lush vineyards and be able to walk up and down the rows and pick the grapes. Libra is also olive oil season, so you press the olives into oil. So aside from law and judgment, when you hear wine, grapes, winepress, vineyard or olive oil, or oil, they're talking about Libra. Next Scorpio is the scorpion, and he's known as the betrayer. When a scorpion bites you, it leaves an imprint in your skin that looks like a pair of lips. It's why the mafia has the kiss of death. This is why Jesus was betrayed by Judas with a kiss. Each zodiac sign correlates to one of the Zodiac signs, I'll give you another example later. So the Sun is judged in Libra, betrayed in Scorpio and finally in Sagittarius this is where the bow and the arrow shoot the Sun and inflict further punishment on the Sun killing it. I mentioned early December 21st which is the 'day of death.'

Any death in the Bible or ancient holy text referring to death refers metaphorically to this date. So when you hear horse, bow and arrow, spear, horseman, and I'll explain the spear later, they're talking about Sagittarius. Basically, you have to remember 'death' for Sagittarius. Then finally we come to Capricorn, the Goat. If you look at the Zodiac wheel, Capricorn is at the bottom of it. If you superimpose a dot at the very bottom, and picture it walking alongside the Zodiac, going up a degree a day it metaphorically is 'starting the climb up the mountain.' And who better that climbs the mountain than the goat. Have you ever seen a Goat climb a one foot ledge all the way up the mountain?' I paused as I saw people in the crowd nodding their heads, 'nobody climbs it better than the goat'. And it's really that simple folks." I finished.

"Now, all you need to do is remember all the key words for each sign and the next parts will make complete sense. Now, there are words or rather names that are given to Jesus from the church that are astrology based that NOBODY knows better about. Remember the key words. Now, when Jesus/the SUN is in Capricorn, the goat, he's called 'the scapegoat of Israel.' When he's in Aquarius the sign of the man, he's 'the Son of man,' when he's in Pisces, the two fish, he's 'the fisherman of men,' it's also why he could feed the masses with 2 fish. When he's in Aries he's 'the Lamb of God, or the Good Shepherd. When he's in Leo he's 'Lion of Judah.' When he's in Virgo which is the virgin holding the stalk of wheat, he's 'born of a virgin and he's called the bread of life. When he's in Libra, he's known as the 'just one.' He's betrayed in Scorpio, he dies in Sagittarius (December 21st) and it's why he's worshipped on the SUNday. Whereas the Jewish religion has roots in Saternalia worship which is why they worship on the SATURNday or the Saturday. It's also why people wear wedding RINGS, because of the rings of Saturn. They were told to make their vow to their spouse in front of their God. It's also why women wear EARRINGS. Again, the rings. They were told to listen to their God. Saturn was once our second Sun and used to be much closer to us than it is now, but that's a conversation for another day," I paused.

"Now, look at this picture of Jesus that I ripped from the internet. It's a standard cartoon drawing of him. You'll always see 4 things in any picture you have of him. You'll see the sun behind his head, the two fingers up, the heart outside the body, and that stereotypical white face of him," I paused to take another sip of water. "The sun is always behind Jesus because he represents the Sun. They did the same with Horus, the Sun God in ancient Egypt. Sometimes there's a Knights Templar cross in the Sun. The two fingers up are an ancient Khemetic peace sign. Khem being Egyptian. We get the words Alchemy, Chemistry, Kemetism, Kemetic, from it. The John Lennon peace sign is actually an ancient British victory war sign. The fingers are separate and make a V for Victory. So, whenever you see Baphomet or Jesus or Buddha or any ancient Gods putting them up, they're telling you they come in peace. Now, the white Jesus picture, his face is actually a guy named Cesare Borgia who was the bastard son of Pope Alexander the 6th. Popes used to have kids, but they were all bastards because they could never marry. Rodrigo Borgia, from the elite Borgia family, bought his way to the papacy in the mid 1500's and decided his sons face would be the face of Jesus. Another thing happened in the mid 1500's which helped spread this. The printing press came out, which to this day is the greatest invention we've ever come up with. It helped spread his face. Now it wasn't like the Muslims where you're not allowed to draw Mohammed,' I said as my focus went back to the man in the front row whose face went from smiling to an angered frown, 'It was just that before him there was no face for him. Now lastly you see the heart outside the body with the crown of thorns. Why does nobody ever question why the heart is on the outside of the body in every picture. Peculiar. The crown of thorns represent the rays of the Sun. Jesus is crucified with a crown of thorns on his head, the crown represents the rays. The heart outside the body represents the toroidal field or the TAURUS field. For those who don't know what that is, it's an electromagnetic field of the heart that circumvents you six feet outside your body. That's why during that great pandemic, they tried to keep you six feet apart. They said nobody could answer why, but this was the reason. To think about it plainly, it resembles an apple, with your body being the core of the apple. When you're within 6 feet of someone, your hearts are communicating esoterically with one another. When someone comes up behind you and you just know someone is there, it's not because you're a wizard, it's because they broke your field. Some people call it an aura, there are different words for that. OK, now that we have gotten through this so far, let's start decoding some phrases.

"Proverbs 16:18, 'Pride comes before the fall.' Now many people take that to mean that your ego will be your downfall if you get too boastful. However, in Astrology a group of lions is called a Pride. Pride is the Lion, the Lion is Leo, Leo is in July/August, that comes before the fall." I said as I looked around the arena. I wasn't really able to see past the first few rows because of the lights. "Now next, in Micah 5:2, the prophet Micah predicts that the savior will come from a town called Bethlehem. 'But you, Bethlehem Ephrathat, though you are small among the clans of Judah, out of you will come for me one who will be ruler over Israel, whose origins are from of old, from ancient times.' However, to understand this you have to know your Hebrew. Throughout this presentation you will need to know your Hebrew, your Italian, your Greek and your English. Bethlehem is a combination of two Hebrew words. Bet which means house, and Lehem which means bread. So the House of Bread. Each Zodiac sign is called a house or a mansion or an aeon. In the Bible Jesus says in my fathers home there are many mansions. So the House of Bread is Virgo, the lady with the wheat stalk, the virgin. So when Micah is saying that the savior is coming from Bethlehem, he's really saying that the savior comes from a virgin," I said.

"Now, the next one will open everything up for you. Deuteronomy 32. Let's see if you can catch all the signs, I'll emphasize them for you. 'He gave them *honey* from the cliffs and **olive oil** from the rocky ground. He gave his people butter from the herd and *milk* from the flock. He gave them **lambs** and **goats**. They had the best **rams** from Bashan and the finest **wheat**. They drank the best **wine** made from the juice of **red grapes**. But Jeshurun became fat and kicked like a **bull**. If you're counting you probably counted 8 so far. There are 2 I didn't mention but will explain. Olive oil is Libra as I've mentioned, the lambs are Aries, and the goat is Capricorn. The rams are Aries, and the wheat is Virgo with the wheat stalk. The wine and the red grapes are Libra as well and the bull is Taurus. 7 lines and 8 signs. However, there are two more. The honey from the cliffs. In the sign of Cancer, there is a group of stars called the beehive cluster. It's an asterism or a short-knit group of stars. The honey comes from them. The milk comes from the Milky Way Galaxy, which was referred to by name as far back as the Egyptian Book of the Dead. The Milky Way Galaxy center is in Sagittarius. So your land from Cancer to Sagittarius is your promised land of 'Milk and Honey.' It's not a place on Earth, it's in the Heavens."

"Next is the Mount of Olives. Jesus led his disciples to the Mount of Olives after his last Passover so that he could teach them a few more things, pray, then wait for Judas to betray him. While walking to the Mount of Olives, he gave the parable of the True Vine," I paused and reached in my pocket and grabbed a CBD joint from a pack and lit it up. I no longer smoked cigarettes. I decided when my boy was born that I actually wanted to be around long enough for him to wipe my ass one day. The arena started to smell a bit like pot, and everyone cheered. "Relax guys, this is only CBD," I said. "Now where were we? Oh yes. OK, so for this one follow the Zodiac wheel that you see on the projector. Passover takes place in Aries as I've mentioned during the 12 signs, where right after he walks to the Mount of Olives. Olives are in Libra. Aries and Libra are opposing signs. I'm sure you guys are sick to death of me talking about this, but it's always going to be talking about a connecting sign or an opposing or 'cross' sign. The Bible is full of these patterns. OK so they are in Libra and waiting for Judas to betray him. Well, the betrayal happens in Scorpio, the betrayer remember? So they're still in Libra and he gives the parable of the True Vine, or Wine or Libra. So first it goes across the wheel, then the next sign over, then back to Libra, and finishes off in Libra. Now, the next passage is from Revelation," I said.

"Revelation 4:7. 'The first living creature was like a lion, the second was like an ox, the third had a face like a man, the fourth was like a flying eagle. There are people on this planet that actually believe this is a real four headed beast that will show up. However, astrology tells a different story. The first living creature was like a lion or Leo. The second was like an Ox or Taurus. The third had a face like a man or Aquarius, the sign of the man. The fourth was like a flying eagle. In astrology, the scorpio/scorpion is the belly crawling creature and is the lowest form of life on Earth because of it. Much like the snake in the garden of Eden after the deception is made to slither on their belly as a demeaning punishment. Now, the Scorpions evolved form in Astrology is the Eagle, and the Eagle evolves once more into the Phoenix. What is the story of the Phoenix? It's a flaming ball, much like Jesus the SUN of God, that dies, and is re-born. So the Scorpio becomes the Eagle. Leo/Taurus/Aquarius/Scorpio are the four fixed signs of the Zodiac. In Astrology you have things called Fixed signs, Mutable or Cardinal signs. The reason these four are fixed is because they're fixed in their seasons. Leo is the dead of summer, Taurus is the dead of spring, Aquarius is the dead of winter and Scorpio/Eagle is the dead of fall. But that's not all. Watch this," I said as I took my laser pointer out and traced a line from Leo to Aquarius and Taurus to Scorpio, "These signs are all opposing signs. They make an X through the Zodiac wheel. So I ask you all, which explanation is more likely? A four headed creature, or this science that works."

"Revelation 12. 'A great sign appeared in heaven: a woman clothed with the sun, with the moon under her feet and a crown of twelve stars on her head. She was pregnant and cried out in pain as she was about to give birth. Then another sign appeared in heaven: an enormous red dragon with seven heads and ten horns and seven crowns on its heads. Its tail swept a third of the stars out of the sky and flung them to earth. So, a woman clothed with the Sun is a metaphor for the Sun being in Virgo. The Virgin is 'clothed' by the appearance of the Sun. If the Sun is in Virgo, the Moon will be at 'her feet.' So, we have 12 Zodiac signs and a 24 hour a day clock. The Sun spends 2 hours a day in each sign, makes sense, simple math. If the Sun is in Virgo that's around 4-6 PM, so the Sun is still out. If the Sun is out, the Moon is 'at her feet' and if the Moon is out, the Sun is at her feet, another metaphor. Then another sign appeared in Heaven. An enormous Dragon. Its tail swept a third of the stars out of the sky and flung them to Earth. The constellation Draco is the Dragon. Its tail goes from Aries to Sagittarius which is 4/12 or 1/3 of the stars out of the sky. Again, what's more realistic, a giant Dragon facing off against a pregnant woman in the sky, or this that makes way more sense.

"Matthew 10:16, 'Behold, I send you forth as sheep in the midst of wolves.' The sheep is Aries as I've mentioned, and the wolf is the constellation Lupus who borders the Libra line. Those are OPPOSING SIGNS." I said as I took a deep drag of my joint.

"Now, I've given you examples of Astrotheology in the Old Testament, as well as the New Testament. I've been accused of cherry picking verses on my

Aquastream channel, in my book series, even though I literally took that from my own life experience the past 10 years. Let's take a much longer passage and see if we can decode it as well." I said as I snubbed out the joint and took a sip of water. I was feeling relaxed, despite 20,000 people all there watching me talk. All except this one guy in the front row. He was making me a bit nervous.

"Excuse me sir, what's your name?" I asked.

The guy looked to his right and his left and pointed to himself.

"Yes you." I said.

"Ibrahim." He replied.

"Well Ibrahim I need your help. Do you know who Job was?" I asked.

He nodded.

"Get him a mic," I said to the crew. "Would you please tell everyone who Job was?" I asked.

He took a second. "Job was a righteous man who had everything. The love of his family, wealth, money, animals, children. One day God was tested by Satan who told him that the only reason he is loyal is because he has everything. If you were to take it all away, he'd curse you. God took the bet. He did tell Satan that he could do anything he wanted to him, except take his life. Little by little animals got sick and ran away, his family started dying, he lost his money. At one point he looks up to Heaven and cries out to God asking him why this all happened." He said as I cut him off.

"Stop right there. Thank you, Ibrahim. So, what I'm going to read to you next is God's response to Job. The first sentence will be what's in the Bible, the second is the decoding. Remember two things. One, is that the book of Job is the oldest book in the Bible, it actually predates Genesis. It wasn't put in its proper place until the council of Jamnia which happened in 100 AD, but is irrelevant now, I've talked about it to death on my podcasts. The second is that not only is the Bible about the 12 Zodiac signs, but also the constellations they knew about at the time and individual stars. See, in our neck of the woods in the universe there are 88 constellations that we know of. But at the ancient time these books were written, they only knew of 48 of them. So, let's begin. First God says, 'Can you lead forth the Mazzaroth?' Now, it's important to know that the Mazzaroth literally means the Zodiac. So God's first challenge to him is asking him if he knows his Zodiac. Mazzaroth over time becomes the Mazalot, which survives in Judaism today as mazel tov which means 'good fortune from the stars', and we all know how old Mazel Tov goes back. So what is the Lord's challenge to Job. 'Can you bind the chains of the Pleiades? Can you loosen

Orion's Belt?' Well, those two are obvious star challenges, metaphorized of course. But what's the next one? 'Can you bring forth the constellations in their seasons or lead out the bear with its cubs?' The constellations are the Zodiac above; the bear and its cubs are Ursa Major, the Great Bear, and Ursa Minor, part of the Big Dipper. Then he says, 'Who can tip over the water jars of the heavens?' Well, that's obviously Aquarius, the man with the water pitcher tipping it over. 'Do you hunt the prey for the lioness and satisfy the hunger of the lions?' That's Leo the Lion. 'Who provides food for the raven?' The constellation Corvus, which means raven and borders on Virgo. 'Do you watch where the doe bears her fawn?' Mriga, meaning deer, is located in Orion. 'Who let the wild donkey go free?' Asellus Borealis meaning donkey and is located in Cancer. 'Will the wild ox consent to serve you?' The bull Taurus. Do you all see where I'm going with this?" I asked as pockets of applause rang through the modern-day coliseum. 'The wings of the ostrich flap joyfully,' Lambda Aquilae or Al Thalimain, which means 'two ostriches' in Arabic. 'Do you give the horse its strength? It laughs at fear, afraid of nothing; it does not shy away from the sword, the quiver rattles against its side, along with the flashing SPEAR and lance.' Sagittarius with the bow and the arrow. Sagittarius means death remember. The spear does as well, the spear can be referred to as Sagittarius as I've previously mentioned. If I were to ask you what the two most important murders are in the Bible, most of you would say Jesus. Well, Jesus is hit in the side of his body with the 'spear of destiny' to check to make sure he's dead. But what else? Well, how about the FIRST murder? Cain and Abel. Sure, Cain hit him over the head with a rock and buried him, but if you know your Hebrew, the word Cain means Spear. The Spear is the weapon of death. Almost done, don't worry guys. 'Does the eagle soar at your command and build its nest on high? 'Aquila is the Latin name for Eagle and is a constellation a few degrees above the celestial equator. But wait, some of you are asking yourself, isn't Scorpio the Eagle? It has multiple meanings. Real quick, just another example would be the constellation Hydra, which is the serpent and Ophiuchus which is the Serpent and the Serpent Bearer. Finally, 'Can you pull in Leviathan with a fishhook,' That's Pisces. I paused and took a fresh bottle of cold water from the ice bucket I had written into my rider when I perform.

"So, questions at the beginning. How was Jesus able to heal the blind? Well, if he's the SON of God, the blind man walked up to him, he touched his eyes and the man was able to see. But the Sun does that too. When it's dark outside we are blind so to speak, we can't see.

206

When the Sun rises in the morning and touches our eyes, we are given the gift of sight back. How he walked on water. Have you ever seen a sunset on a lake before? The Sun literally walks across it. How he turned water into wine. This is a little more complicated. The reason that God is considered a man and Earth mother Earth a woman forever throughout cultures has to do with God's sacred fluid. The rain. In Hebrew the word is She-men, we get the word semen from it. So God's sacred fluid pours down onto mother earth and from her belly, fruit, plants, trees, vegetation et cetera grow from it. So you put the plow on the Bull in Taurus, April showers bring May flowers remember, that's in Taurus, and it rains throughout until you pick the grapes in Libra, press them and turn them to wine. From a seed to wine. Watered by God. That's how you turn water into wine. Why he had 12 disciples? Each one of them represents a specific Zodiac sign. I've already told you that Scorpio the betrayer is Judas. One other example is Pisces. Simon Peter. Now my name is Graham, sometimes people call me G, my wife called me asshole, whatever you know. Thomas is Tom, Patrick is Pat, Antonia is Toni. But why Simon to Peter? Makes no sense, unless you know your astrology. Simon's job was a fisherman, and the fish are the two fish in Pisces. So what's the ruling planet of Pisces? It's Jupiter or Jew Peter. Why was he betrayed with a kiss by Judas, we went over that, why was he dead for 3 days, we went over that, why is his birthday on December 25th, we went over that." I paused and took another sip of water. These lights are boiling hot. I hope they're all having a good time.

"Now, Jesus disappears at 12 and comes back at 30. There are plenty of explanations for that, but historically and astrologically they make the most sense. First astrologically there are 12 signs of 30 degrees in the Zodiac wheel. But even if you don't want to accept that, there's another one. What happens to a young Jewish boy at the age of 12? He becomes Bar Mitzvah'd. He becomes a 'man' in the eyes of Judaism. So Jesus becomes a man and leaves to study. He starts his ministry at 30. Why 30? As I've mentioned before, the Jewish religion has its roots in Saturnalia worship. It's why they worship on the Saturnday or Saturday. Saturnalia worshippers said that you were not allowed to become a teacher until Saturn came back to the point it was at when you were born. If you know your astrology, you know that Saturn takes 30 years to circle around the Sun one time. That's why he disappeared at 12 and reappeared at 30.

"Now you have to understand that I believe in God, but not the God of the ancient holy texts. My view of God is a combination of two theories. One is that God is infinite, and nothing can exist outside of infinity, so we are all part of God experience itself subjectively. Combine that with what Einstein said about Spinoza's view on God and you have it. To me, God exists through Astrology. The Sun tells the hour of the day, the moon tells the day of the month, and the zodiac tells the month of the year. The chances of a perfect celestial calendar to happen through a big bang or some nonsense is not just idiotic to me, it's offensive." I thumped.

"Now, Moses goes up to get the 10 commandments and when he comes down, he sees them worshipping a Golden Calf. So, I ask you all what's more likely? The Jews got run out of Egypt, that they couldn't even let the bread rise, which is why we have matzah to this day. They rushed to the desert with just the clothes on their back but happened to carry enough gold between all of them, found welding equipment in the desert and built a giant statue, or, the Sun is the Gold and the Calf is the Bull or Taurus. They were worshipping the Sun in Taurus, whereas they are the Jews or the people of Aries. Now, the ancient Egyptians used to worship the Sun in Taurus. Heiroglyphs of the Bull with the Sun between its horns, it's obvious if you know what you're looking at. Now the Jews are the people of Aries, that's why they blow the ram's horn to the sky on the holidays. Now, Christians are the people of Pisces, that's why they have the Jesus fish which is taken when you take the center of the Vesica PISCES. This is also why Jesus is able to feed the masses with 2 fish. John 21 'So Simon Peter climbed back into the boat and dragged the net ashore. It was full of large fish, 153, but even with so many, the net was not torn.' 153, seems like a random number, doesn't it? Remember the Vesica Pisces we were just talking about? Its mathematical equation is 247/153. Do you think there are things the ancients knew that were worth encoding in a book?" I asked as I took a huge gulp of the water.

"Genesis 32:30. 'And Jacob called the name of the place Peniel, for I have seen God face to face, and my life is preserved.' Well, Peniel, is just Pineal over time. For those that don't know what the Pineal Gland is, it's a small pinecone shaped gland, hence where it gets its name from that sits in the base of the brain. It has two primary functions. The first is to produce melatonin which is naturally produced when the Sun goes down, in order to prepare you for sleep. It's second function is that it produces DMT. For those that don't know what DMT is, it's Dimethyltriptamine which is a potent hallucinogen. It floods your body many times through your life but only on two occasions. The first one is as you're in heavy REM sleep, and it causes you to dream, visit other dimensions, parallel universes, what have you. The second time it's produced is as your body is shutting down to die, your brain floods your body with this. Possibly as a way to prepare you for the afterlife, who knows. Now, in many Buddhist traditions, 49 days is the total mourning period, with prayers conducted every 7 days, across 7 weeks. These Buddhists believe that rebirth takes place within 49 days after death. Fast forward thousands of years, it just so happens that the Pineal Gland becomes visible on the 49th day of gestation. It is the seat of our soul, and many people who run things don't want you to know how powerful you truly are, they try and keep you down with your religious wars with each other. All you religious people, you all believe in the same God, and the same Satan, however you fight about the messenger. That's like going to a restaurant with your friends but fighting over which waitress you want." I paused and looked around. "It's ok, because we're coming up to the point of the night shortly where I go over the one thing I've never gone over before, and because it's my last show I'm doing for a long time, I'm going to show you all the Astrology in the Koran." I said. People started clapping, there were some groans in the crowd. I looked down to my friend in the front row again and this time he looked furious. Oh man, we were doing so good, he was in such a good mood after I asked him that question about Job. "We'll get there people, just let me get through a couple more things." I pleaded.

"Now, the idea of Hell being a flaming inferno. How do we sense pain? Through the nervous system. The brain, spinal cord, nerve endings. So, let me ask you a question. When we give up our ghost and lose the brain and the nervous system, how would we be able to as a soul, BURN? The idea of a fiery pit where you burn for all eternity is ridiculous when you think about it logically. The truth is that hell is literally WINTER on Earth. Why? It's cold, the vegetation and beautiful flowers and plants are dead; the trees shed their leaves and bear no fruit. It's freezing cold out. People tend to get sick more often. Dangerous animals if they're not hibernating are starving and scrounging for food. It's dangerous for humans. Now, the Italian word for winter is INVERNO. You flip a letter and flip the meaning and you get the concept of hell. In Dante Aligheris the 'Divine Comedy,' Satan is in the bottom level of hell. He is frozen up to his waist in a frozen tundra, because his wings are flapping so hard that it's freezing everything over. Dante knew hell was winter on Earth. My question is why don't you?" I said as I paused and cracked another water bottle. Now, continuing with Satan and Lucifer, Satan doesn't actually exist. He's not a red devil with a tail and a pitchfork, in fact in the earliest paintings of him in the 900's, he was actually blue, not red. The Hebrew word for Satan is HASHATAN which literally translates to adversary. In proper contect, two competing sports teams are Satan's to one another. Well, what about Lucifer? He is known as the light bearer. In Genesis 1.3 'And God said let there be light.' Well, how can there be light without the light bringer? Lucifer is immediately mentioned in the Bible if not by name, but by action and purpose. Lucifer is also known as the Morningstar. The Morningstar is also known as the planet Venus. The reasoning is that if you go out and look at the sky just before the Sunrise, you will see a bright light directly over it. Every day you will see this. That's Venus, it announces the arrival of 'God's only begotten Sun, the 'light' of the world.' Lucifer is also known the have a pentagram, that's his symbol. Continuing with Lucifer as Venus, if you follow Earth and Venus's orbit around the Sun in a year's time, they almost connect at 5 points. You connect those points you get the pentagram."

"It's not just these stories though. It's EVERY story in the Bible that has to do with astrology or the Sun. Samson and Delilah. The root word in Hebrew of Samson is Shemesh, which means Sun. Samson literally means 'little sun.' In Hebrew the word Shamash is used to represent the candle that you light in the Hannukah

Menorah that lights all the other candles. It's a representation of the Sun bringing light and illumination to the rest of the world. Now, Delilah, the root word of Delilah is Lilah. Lilah means 'night.' What happens to Samson? He gets his hair cut and loses his powers, he goes blind and cannot see. This story is a metaphor for the night overtaking the day. It's the eternal battle that the Egyptians called between Horus and Set. That's why we have a 'sunset' to this day."

"What about Jonah and the whale? In Hebrew the words are Dag Gadol which translates to Great/Giant fish. This is representative of Pisces, the fish. He's in the fish for 3 days. Again, here we see the recurring 3 days over and over again, which goes back to the Sun walking sideways like the crab for 3 days in December. When the 'Sun' dies for 3 days, just like Jonah was dead for 3 days."

"What about Daniel and the Lion's den? It's a story of Daniel who's represented by the man sign of Aquarius in a Lion's Den with Lions. The Lions are Leo. Aquarius and Leo are opposing signs."

"There's a town in Israel called Megiddo which a 3rd century Church was found underneath another church. It's one of the oldest Churches known to man. In the center of the floor is the mosaic of the 2 fish, Pisces. The ancients knew they were the people of Pisces, and they showed it back then. The word Megiddo is also the root of the word Armageddon, which is where the war on Earth and the rapture is supposed to begin."

"The Swastika, if you read on the internet, is a hateful symbol. Some people know that it comes from a peaceful symbol of ancient times. Again, invert it and pervert it and you get the modern day meaning that we will never reclaim to be a peaceful symbol. However, what most people know is that it goes further back than that. The Swastika isn't Buddhist, or Hindu, Babylonian, or Syrian or Sumerian. It's actually Astrology. The oldest swastika that we've found is 17,000 years old and it's from the Ukraine. So, what is the swastika? If you take a snapshot of the big dipper as it rotates around Polaris on the solstices and equinoxes, it forms a swastika."

"But this all goes further than that. How is astrology being used in modern day things. Well, the basketball team the Phoenix Suns is one example. The Phoenix is the story of Christ the SUN. A flaming form of life, that dies and rises from its ashes metaphorically. That's why Phoenix is the SUNS. What about the woman's Phoenix team? They're called the Phoenix Mercury. Mercury being the ruling planet of Virgo, the sign of the woman. How else are modern day things encoded? 1990's movie 'Face Off' starring Nicolas Cage and John Travolta.

What are the names of the characters? Nicolas Cage is Castor Troy and his brother is Pollux Troy. Those are the names of Gemini! What about Travolta? His name is Sean Archer. Archer being the man with the bow and the arrow. Those are OPPOSING SIGNS. So what else? 1990's song video for the Cranberries Zombie. Dolores O'Riorden in the video is painted gold like the Sun and her head dressings represents the rays of the Sun, much like Jesus and the crown of thorns? Well, the very next scene is her, gold in all on a cross with a bunch of young adolescents with the bow and arrow pointing at her. This represents Sagittarius killing the Sun on the Cross of God's Son/Sun. In Katy Perry's 'Dark Horse' video, you can see that she has the eye of Horus painted on her eye. This draws attention to the eye, which in modern day conspiracy worlds is the 'all seeing eye,' however, in reality it is the Eye of Horus which represents the Pineal gland, which is knowledge and a portal to other dimensions. Now, what are some other modern-day things that revolve around astrology. How about mermaids? It's a combination of the woman sign Virgo and the fish sign Pisces. What about Mermen? Aquarius the man and Pisces the fish. Those two are CONNECTING SIGNS on the Zodiac. What about Bullfighting or bull riding? That's Aquarius the man and Taurus the Bull. What about jousting? That's 2x Sagittarius. What about Lion

Taming? That's Aquarius the man and Leo the Lion. Those are OPPOSING SIGNS. What about fishing? That's Aquarius the man and Pisces the Fish. Those are CONNECTING SIGNS," I paused as I looked out into the audience. "We're going to take a quick break in a few there's just one more thing I wanted to talk about before we get into the Koran for the second half." I said.

"HOMOSEXUALITY IN THE BIBLE!" I shouted as people started to boo. "Everybody knows about Leviticus 18.22. However, is that all that there is to it? The Greek word 'Arsenokoitai' shows up in 2 different versions of the Bible in Greek but was not translated to mean 'homosexual' until 1946. In the 1800's the German Bible said, "Man shall not lie with young boys as he does with a woman, for it is an abomination.' Leviticus 18.22, same with Leviticus 20.13. 1 Corinthians the word Arsenokoitai, and it's important to mention that the Bible was written in Hebrew, but everybody at the time knew that if you were an intellect, you wrote and read in Greek. So, 1 Corinthians becomes 'Boy molesters will not inherit the kingdom of God.' If you were to grab Martin Luther's original German translation from 1534, they used the word knabenschander. Knaben is boy, schander is molester. The first time homosexual appears in German translation is in 1983." I paused to take another gulp of water.

"We're going to take a quick break, but I just wanted to tell you that I've decoded the following books with Astrotheology. The ones that are biblical or gnostic texts are the Book of Matthew, Revelation, Enoch, Jubilees, Thomas, Mary Magdeline, Melchizedek, Philip and Judas. However, it doesn't stop there. It's not just biblical texts. The other ancient texts that I've decoded are the Emerald Tablets of Thoth, the Enuma Elish, Epic of Gilgamesh, Code of Hammurabi, Egyptian Book of the Dead, and finally the Koran. When you get back, we'll start on the Koran." I said as I walked my way backstage and sat down in a chair.

It felt so good to finally get this out. I had presented this work to the grand lodge in Manhattan. I reached out to them after Josh had passed and told them everything. They had cut a decent part of it out when they converted it to film, but people were still reading my books, and they wanted me to present to them. My presentation went into their library. I'm not going to lie, I felt like a young Manly P. Hall when I was presenting to them. I decided to present all this in my hometown arena before I took a break from it all. After about 10 minutes I heard some noise from the crowd. I guess they had peed, gotten another beer, went out for a cigarette, what have you. I had never presented the following information to anybody, and I was glad that so many people packed the coliseum to see me fight the lions and give everyone bread and wine. I lit up another CBD joint and went back out to roaring applause.

"OK everyone, now as I previously mentioned, they said not to film this, but I don't care. I want you to share this with everyone you know," I began. "Let's begin. Sura 1. The opener of the book. 'Day of Judgment One He is the sovereign.' The day of Judgment is December 21st in Sagittarius, which is when the Sun is finally executed on the Judgment provided during Libra, the scales, the just one. Sura 2. The Cow. 'When they are told: 'You on earth do not sow wickedness,' They answer: "On the contrary! We only sow good here." The sowing takes place during Taurus, which is when you plant the seeds. It's a metaphor. 22. He raised up the heavens as a covering, and poured out water (abundantly) from heaven, to grow fruit for your food. The Zodiac is the heavens covering. Pouring out water come from Aquarius, the man with the water pitcher pouring it out. 25 They are waiting for Gardens, washed by rivers. And whenever they will be served fruits from there. The rivers are Pisces, the river with the fish in them and they will be served fruits in Libra, when the fruits are ready to be harvested. 29 Then he proceeded to (create) the heavens and in them he built seven celestial vaults. The seven 'vaults' are the 7 planets they knew about at the time. Up until recently we had 9 planets, now we're down to 8. Not including Nibiru, which is another lecture altogether. But they only knew of 7. 51 You, in his absence too, the Taurus for veneration. 54 You, having taken a calf (for veneration). This is talking about the Bull in Taurus, openly talking about it. 93 Hold fast to what was entrusted to you and follow obediently (this law) They answered, 'We hear, but we do not obey him' out of their unbelief, they poured out into their hearts a perverse affection for the calf. The law is Libra, the law and judgment. They poured their hearts the affection for the calf. The calf is the Bull. They were worshiping the Bull again. However, they were in the age of Pisces. This was wrong. I draw back your attention to the story of the Golden Calf from earlier. It is said that when the third temple is to be built in Israel, a slaughter of a PERFECT bull must be performed. It must be combed to make sure there are no miscolored hairs. This is back to Bull worship, which everyone is so eager to go back to, but is incorrect. I didn't get into this, but I believe that since we are in the Age of Aquarius, the sign of the man, it's the age where the man becomes elevated. In 1500 years they will look back and see the new religion that formed during this time period, however my best guess right now is that the new religion will be merging with machines. But that's for another day. 118 Those who do not know say: Why has not the Lord turned the Word to us and why will he not show us a sign from heaven? Similar words were spoken by those who came before them, their hearts are alike. We interpret the signs for those who are committed to their faith (with all their soul). This is talking about looking for a sign in Heaven. They're literally talking about God showing them a sign or interpreting it for them. They interpret the signs for those who are committed to faith. Other people understanding the zodiac than you." I paused to take a sip of the diet Snapple I got from the back. "164 Verily, in the creation of the heavens and the firmament, and in the change (darkness) of the night (light) of the day, and in the ships crossing the seas according to the needs of man, In the rain that Allah pours from heaven and earth that has fallen from death lives on them. In every living creature he scatters over the earth, in motion and change of winds, that clouds between heaven and earth as they drive their servants, truly, here are the hidden signs for those who understand. The Heavens are the zodiac. The living creatures are the fish (Pisces), the lambs and the ram (Aries), the Bull (Taurus), the crab (Cancer), the Lion (Leo) the scorpion and the belly crawling creatures (Scorpio) and the horses (Sagittarius). Truly, here are hidden signs for those who understand. 213 On the day of the Lord's Judgment, He sent the Book of Truth with them, so that people judge among themselves all that diverged (their passions) when clear signs appear to them. The judgment day is December 21st. The Koran was sent for people to judge (Libra) amongst themselves when these CLEAR SIGNS appeared to them. 239 But if you are in danger, pray on foot, or do not dismount from your horse; when the danger has passed you, you call on the Lord with praise. How he taught you and how until then you did not know. Dismounting the horse is Sagittarius. Don't dismount is a way of saying don't fear Sagittarius, the day of death, because the danger will pass, and the Sun will come back to life on December 25th. 266 And whoever wants to own a beautiful garden of date palms and vines, which is washed by abundant streams. Where for his pleasure all kinds of fruits, while old age befalls him, and the children are weak, so that a fiery whirlwind falls on the garden and swallows it to ashes. So the Lord explains his signs to you so that you can understand. Vines are Vineyards in Libra, and the streams are the screams in the water sign of Pisces and Aquarius. God explains these 12 signs to you so that you can understand. Sura 3 The Imran Family, 14, And how beautifully all people see the love of earthly passions: Here are women and sons, there are mountains of silver and gold, and marked horses, and herds of cattle and a plowed field. Women are Virgo the sign of the woman, the sons are Gemini, the brothers. Horses are Sagittarius. Gemini and Sagittarius are OPPOSING SIGNS. The cattle is Taurus. A plowed field is Taurus as well." I paused to compose myself. I'd never given a lecture this long.

"113 But among them there are those who are not like these. Among the people of the Scripture there are those who with patient steadfastness (for the truth) stand and surrendering with all their soul to Allah, spends long hours in the night reading his signs. The signs are the 12 signs of the Zodiac and the key words that I've given you are words in each sign that you need to know to be able to decode these books. 190 Verily, in the creation of earth and sky and in the change of night to day, here are the hidden signs for those who have intelligence. The hidden signs are the Zodiac. 195 The lord heard them (calls) and replied: I will never give to the abyss not a single human deed whether it is a man or a virgin. The man sign is Aquarius the man and the Virgin is Virgo. When they talk about meeting the Virgins in Heaven, well the Virgin in Heaven is Virgo the Virgin. Sura 5 Meal. 64, until the day of their resurrection (at the judgment) and whenever they light the fire of war, the Lord will put it out. The Judgment happens in Libra, on September 21st, the fire of war comes from the God of War, Mars who's the ruling planet of Aries. Those are OPPOSING SIGNS. Sura 6 Cattle, 25, and among them there are those who (only pretendingly) listen to you. We put a cover on their hearts so that they would not understand it. And we covered their ears with deafness. And even if they see all the signs, they will not believe them. The signs are in the Heavens, the 12 Zodiac signs. 97 he is the one who placed the stars (for your needs) to show you the way. When darkness falls on land or see (descends) thus we clarify our signs for those in whom knowledge lives. They're literally talking about understanding the signs in the sky. It's OPENLY talking about it in this passage. 99 He is the one who brings down water to you from the sky. And with it we give plants of all kinds to grow, and with it we grow shoots of cereals, from them we grew grains. Sitting (in an ear of a dense) side by side. From the date palms, its ovaries, bunches of fruits hanging low, gardens of vines, olives, pomegranates which (in many ways) are so similar and yet so different from each other! When fruits appear on them, rejoice in how they are poured and ripen! Truly, in this are hidden signs for those who believed (in God). Well, the grains are planted in Taurus, then April showers bring may flowers, water from the sky, the grains grow. Reap in Virgo. Gardens of Vines and Olives. Grapes and Olives are pressed in Libra. These are the hidden signs you need to know. 105 So we interpret our signs to them in different ways, so that they could not say, you (from others) learned this! And so that (the Truth) we clearly explain for those who have knowledge, so follow what your Lord has revealed to you by suggestion. Listen to what they're saying here, for those who have knowledge, follow what the Lord has revealed. Understand your signs, know what you're looking for and you will find." I paused and took a sip of water as I looked out at the crowd. I saw my friend in the front row, Ibrahim, only now he was red as an apple and looked furious. We made eye contact and he stood up, looked around the arena, turned back to me, bowed and started walking away. I paused while he did this as he made his way down the ramp and out. I know this is a lot to process and I lost my mind basically when I first got privy to this information. I continued. "143 Take in pairs eight heads of cattle, two from sheep and two from goats. The cattle are the Ox, Taurus, the sheep are Aries, those are CONNECTING SIGNS and the goat is Capricorn. Sura 7 Obstacles 8, And the Libra will be faithful on that Day. And those whose cup will be heavy, in the delight of paradise dwell. And those whose cup is lightweight, they themselves will doom themselves to destruction because they were lawless in relation to our signs. Libra literally translates to Libra in Arabic. Libra is the judgment, the cup being heavy or light refers to the sins one has to account for. Lawless is another mention of Libra, as Libra is the law. Our signs refer to the signs of the Zodiac. 32, say all these blessings of a neighbor's life, for those who believed in God with all their souls and only for them on the day of Resurrection at the judgment, thus we explain our signs for those in whom understanding lives. The signs are the signs in the sky. They tell you when to plant, when to harvest, when winter is coming. They tell you what season you are in. The Resurrection comes December 25th the day the Sun is resurrected from the dead from the judgment which takes place September 21st which is the fall equinox. This is the explanation for the signs of the times. 107/108/109/110/111. And Musa threw down his rod, and in front of everyone he turned into a serpent. He stretched out his hand and she flashed whiteness before the eyes of all beholding. Then the nobles from the people of Pharoah said, 'This indeed a skilled sorcerer' and he wants to expel you from your land. What is your advice? They answered 'Delay him and his brother and the summoners went through the cities. Musa is Moses. The Serpent is the 13th sign in Sidereal Astrology Ophiuchus which is between Libra and Scorpio (the serpent bearer. Delay him and his brothers are the brothers in Gemini. Sura 10: Yunus. 5, he is the one who made the sun (life-giving) brilliance, established the moon, that light pours in phases. So that you know the number of years. This is talking about the creation of the Sun and the Moon that tells the time as I've previously mentioned the perfect sky clock. 67, he is the one who created the night, so that you can rest, and the day to let you see. Indeed, here are hidden signs for those in whom the desire to hear. This is the same as the Bible. Jesus says for those who have eyes to see and ears to hear, this is what it's talking about. It's the signs of the Heavens above. 101, say (look around) everything in heaven and on earth! And neither the signs, nor those who carry the message can be useful to people who are stubbornly unfaithful. The signs in the sky are not useful to people who do not recognize them. Surah 12: Yusef. 36, and two young men entered the dungeon with him. One of them said: In a dream I saw that I was squeezing wine (from grapes) Another said 'I saw that I was carrying bread on my head. And the birds peck at it. Tell us the meaning (of these dreams) after all, we see that you are one of those who act according to knowledge and kindness. The young men are Gemini, the two men, the wine is Libra, and the bread comes from Virgo, the lady with the wheat stalk. These are CONNECTING SIGNS. Surah 15: Al-Hijr 75, Verily here are hidden signs for those who seek to recognize (the meaning of our signs). The hidden signs are the Zodiac. Surah 16: Bees 5/8. He created cattle, for you, it contains both warmth and every other benefit and from it you will be flesh for food. He created horses for you, mules and donkeys for journeys and for magnificent ceremonies, and he creates for you much of that which you hitherto unknown. So, the cattle is Taurus, the horses are Sagittarius. The donkey is Asellus Borealis, the donkey which is located in Cancer. 11/12 He used it to grow cereals, olives, palms, vines and many other fruits for your food. Indeed, there is a sign here for those who give themselves up to meditation. He subdued you night and day and the Sun and Moon and by his will he put the star in the service of you. Indeed, there is a sign here for those who have intelligence. Olives and vines are libra. That's the 'sign.' Then talks about the Sun and the Moon and the Star in service is Polaris, the Northern Star. These are the signs that speak to you for those who have intelligence. 67, from palm fruits and vines you find good food for yourself and an intoxicating drink. Here verily, is a sign for those who understand. This is the season of Libra, it's a sign for those with understanding. Sura 18: Cave, 60/61. Musa said to his servant I will not retreat until I reach the place of the confluence of the two seas, at least I had to go years. When they reached the confluence of the two seas, they completely forgot about their fish, which directed its way straight to the sea in a wonderful way. This is talking about the confluence of the two seas, or the two 'water' signs used in decoding of Aquarius and Pisces. He's talking about the border between the two of them. When they got there, they forgot about their fish, so we know they're not talking about Pisces anymore but about Aquarius. Sura 19: Maryam 12: and now, when Yahya was born. Yahya is Yeshua/Jesus. Maryam is his mother, Mary. 15: May there be peace to him on the day he was born, on the day he dies, and on the day when he will rise to life again. The day he was born was December 25th, he dies December 21st as explained and he rises to life again December 25th. 20: How can I have a baby she said when no man touched me, and I was not dissolute. The virgin birth goes to Virgo the constellation of the virgin. Sura 21: Prophets. 78: Also, Daoud and his son Suleiman, when they gave judgment on the field which was harmed by the stray sheep belonging to a family from their community, and we ourselves were present at their trial. Daoud and Suleiman is David and Solomon. The Judgment is Libra, the scales of Justice, the sheep is Aries. Those two signs are OPPOSING SIGNS. Sura 47 Muhammad: 15, here is a figurative parable of paradise which was promised to the faithful: In it are rivers of water that will never be spoiled. And rivers of milk that do not change taste. And rivers of wine to delight those who drink, and rivers of honey that are cleared. The rivers of water are Aquarius/Pisces. The rivers of milk are the Milky Way Galaxy whose center is in Sagittarius. The Rivers of wine are Libra, when you press the grapes for the wine and finally the rivers of honey are in Cancer, where the beehive cluster is. Sura 55: The Merciful, 5: he assigned the paths of motion to the sun and the moon, and determined their phases, 6, the stars in the sky and the trees on earth bow their heads before him, 7, he set up the height vault of heaven and by his will he set the scales for measuring good and evil. Once more talking about the Sun and the Moon and their phases. The vault of Heaven the 'scales' is the sign of Libra once again. Sura 85 Towers, 1, in the sign of the sky, the owner of the Zodiac signs, 2, as a sign of the promised day (last judgment). FINALLY, we get open talk about the Zodiac and the creator of it all. Also, the judgment is Libra once again," I paused and dropped my CBD joint into a half empty water bottle. Finally, we come up to the part about the 72 virgins in Heaven. This is another mention of astrology. There is a star called 70 Virginis which is right along Virgo. The sensual pleasures are graphically elaborated by Al-Suyuti who died in 1505. Koranic commentator and polymath. He wrote that 'Each time we sleep with a houri we find her virgin. Besides, the penis of the elected never softens. The erection is eternal; the sensation that you feel each time you make love is utterly delicious and out of this world and were you to experience it in this world you would faint. Each chosen one (Muslim) will marry seventy houris, besides the woman he married on earth.' Well, there's your 70 virgins, plus 1 which is Virgo, plus the one you married on earth. That's the 72 virgins. Now, for those people who will look it up and say 'Graham, 70 Virginis was only discovered in 1996.' Right. These are the same people and sites you look up that say that Saturn was discovered in 1610, not that it hadn't been discovered thousands and thousands of years prior as I've mentioned before. As Narrated by Abu Dawud regarding astrology in the Hadith it is suggested that the Prophet Muhammad stated, 'Whoever seeks knowledge from the stars is seeking one of the branches of witchcraft,' this of which is inherently forbidden in Islam. Now go over to its sister religion the Catholics and Catechism 2116 forbids astrology. Can you really doubt that these holy books are not based on astrology?

"This my friends is the entire Koran. As you can see, it is no different than any of the other sacred texts I've been decoding in my videos, tv appearance, podcasts, writings, books, et cetera. Can you imagine all the bloodshed that's happened throughout all three major religions due to blind faith belief? Early on before I had a book and movie deal, I had self-published a book called "101 reasons why we desperately need religion". In it there was 385 pages of one sentence. Basically 'we don't' over and over again. It was sort of a gag book. That's before I decided to take this seriously. If you're wondering why I wrote 'fiction' even though it's all true is because when you look at books like 1984 from George Orwell, or Brave New World, or 20,000 leagues under the sea, the books that stay with us through time are truth in fiction. If I had just spewed out all this into non-fiction books, you probably would have not picked it up. But this is all REAL ladies and gentlemen. Unless this gets exposed, we're not going to be able to move forth. We'll be stuck in the back and forth between religious and non-religious people. You need to understand the history and know what I'm talking about. Thank you for your time today. I'll leave you with some final words of wisdom. They will call you 'crazy' because you were born with the gift of seeing things differently and that scares them. They will call you 'intense' because you were born with the courage to allow yourself to live and feel fully and that intimidates them. They'll call you 'selfish' because you've discovered that you're the most important thing in your life and that doesn't benefit them. They'll call you 'conspiracy' because you've seen the control and manipulation that systems try to exercise on you and that doesn't suit them. They will call you 'weird' because you don't do the same things as the masses, because you came out of the matrix and created your own reality. They will call you 'absurd' because you have beliefs different from those that have been instilled in us for years. They will call you 'disturbing' because you act in ways outside of the established ones, because you help, because you teach, because you talk about universes and existence. They will call you 'dangerous' because you don't follow the rules and regulations set, because you create your own way of living in your own way and to your liking. They will call you 'deceiver' because you know we live in a universe of infinite possibilities and that everything is possible if you believe it with certainty. They will tag you in many ways, with many judgments, for a long time, but stand firm in yourself, in your desires and being faithful to your essence, because in the end, they will seek you for what you convey, for what you give, for what you are, through your magic. Don't let yourself down by what they will say, create your own path and trust your inner wisdom, if you doubt anything, investigate, if you disagree with no idea no matter how many people believe it, seek it and your truth, wake up and stop believing everything they told you, draw your own conclusions and manifest your true Me, always from love, always from consciousness, thank you for tonight," I finished as the room exploded in applause. Pictures were taken and the flashes were blinding. I stood there like a deer in the headlights for about 30 seconds before I turned around and walked to the back where everyone was waiting for me.

Our ride back to our house was uneventful. When we finally pulled up at the house, we made our way to the front door. I picked out another CBD joint and lit it up.

"Baby come on, you know that I can't stand the smell of that in the house," Hannah said.

"I'm sorry, I'm just full of electricity right now and I need to simmer down a little. This was my first talk in front of a sold-out crowd," I said to her.

"Alright Newsdon, we'll meet you upstairs," Rosette said as she motioned to everyone.

One by one they all went upstairs, Hannah last, closing the door behind her. I sat there facing the door and puffing on my joint. I had apotheosis at this point. I couldn't imagine taking this any further than I already have. I never needed to work again. A coalition had been created to take down all the evil elitists backstage, people were waking up to the truth about religion. I sat there for once completely satisfied. This is how I want to be remembered when I go. That feeling turned on me shortly thereafter.

"Hey Graham!" Someone shouted behind me.

I turned around. It was Ibrahim.

"Ibrahim, why did you leave? I thought you were really enjoying it. How did you find me?" I asked.

He laughed. "First you expose the origins of Islam, now you say that it's nothing but an encoded Astrology book?" he asked.

"I'm sorry Ibrahim, everything I said is true." I replied.

"I'm sorry too Graham." He said as he pulled out a gun from his pocket. My entire body froze.

"Ibrahim, wait," I pleaded. It was no use.

All I felt was a piercing pain in my left chest and then I heard the crack of the gun.

"You can spend your whole life trying to be popular, but at the end of the day, the size of the crowd at your funeral will be largely dictated by the weather," Ibrahim said as he saluted me and took off running, dropping the gun in the sewer about 200 feet from me.

I looked down and saw blood pouring out of my chest. My breathing became labored. I started coughing up blood and hit my knees. I reached out in front of me for something, anything to grab on to. I couldn't breathe at this point and my breaths were incredibly short and labored. I fell onto my face and stared out into the middle of the road. My breathing got slower and slower until everything went black. Then suddenly………

There was nothing.

Coming Soon!

Into the Rabbit Hole
Nail in the Coffin
By Micah T. Dank

Nail in the Coffin, Book Eight, the continuation of *Into the Rabbit Hole*: Will Graham survive or not? It doesn't matter. There is a man that controls the financial destiny of every country on the planet. A long line of 250 years of doing so. He must be stopped before the World devolves into WW III and the destruction of the entire planet.

For more information
visit: www.SpeakingVolumes.us

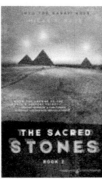

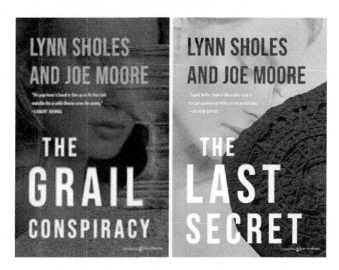

Printed in Great Britain
by Amazon

31128158R00142